LEGAL GROUNDS

AVA AARONSON

BookLocke

Published by BookLocker.com, Inc., St. Petersburg, Florida.

Printed on acid-free paper.

This is a work of fiction. Names, characters, businesses, places, events, locales, and incidents are either the products of the author's imagination or used in a fictitious manner. Any resemblance to actual persons, living or dead, or actual events is purely coincidental.

BookLocker.com, Inc.
2019

First Edition

Cover: *Café Terrace at Night* is an 1888 oil painting by Vincent van Gogh, in the public domain.

Library of Congress Cataloging in Publication Data
Aaronson, Ava
Legal Grounds by Ava Aaronson
FICTION /General | FICTION / Mystery & Detective / General | FICTION / Women
Library of Congress Control Number: 2019904876

TRIGGER OR CONTENT WARNING:

This novel includes graphic descriptions of and extensive discussion of abuse, incest, torture, and personally-inflicted violence as experienced by a child and a young person.

There are also graphic descriptions of and extensive discussion of self-harming behavior including suicide, self-inflicted injuries, and eating disorders.

There are depictions, including lengthy and psychologically realistic ones, of the mental state of someone suffering abuse and then contemplating and engaging in self-harming.

There are instances of forced deprivation and disregard for personal autonomy.

Some of the abuse is done in the name of God and with the reinforcement of certain passages from the Bible. At times, clergy that are informed do not intervene.

DEDICATION

This novel is dedicated to the stalwart men and noble women of every race, religion, region, occupation, socio-economic status and generation, who ethically, sacrificially, humbly, and courageously do the right thing with regard to exploited and missing children.

These are the people who lay down their lives to work at creating a safe community for all, where might is not right, where licentious perversion neither overtly nor covertly rules, and finally, where the agency of one's fellow person is not conquered for another's dominion.

It is also dedicated to the National Center for Missing and Exploited Children.

TABLE OF CONTENTS

PART I

Chapter One
Legal Latté

Friday, October 5th, 5 a.m., Stella texted Ellie: On my way; offer coffee to client. Thx.

What began as a hushed tête-à-tête in a café back office ended in deadly open aggression on the front terrace. The morning opener intern was the first to note the oddity of one particular early morning engagement. Interns, of course, are the ones at the bottom doing the grunt work and taking it all in like a fly on the wall. They appear to know everything about everyone that goes on in their place of training and low wages. No one seems to notice that they are there, and yet interns see and hear everything.

About a month later, likewise, it was the café closer intern that called in the law to clean up the battle aftermath on the front terrace. When it all came down, that intern gave testimony as to what had actually happened. He, too, was so small in the scheme of things that the warring parties went at each other with neither blush nor reserve. He similarly was the shy mouse working behind the counter in the mellow eventide who witnessed the disturbance. The intern could recount every detail; however, no one had noticed that he was present when chaos ignited.

It was not a question of the interns being uninformed or of a low brain capacity. They were actually scholars: local college students studying business. Their career study paths required them to take training at a small business for low pay and school credit. In addition to being smart and homegrown, they were observant and intimately familiar with small town life and the concerned parties. Their job, however, was to focus on and learn how to run a successful small business from the ground up. Unfortunately, this particular chain of events was not about success; it was a question of survival.

In the beginning, it had been another classic Friday morning with the regulars streaming in at the 5 a.m. opening of Legal Grounds Café, craving coffee for their morning runs to work. There were the cabbies and independent drivers headed to airports, delivering riders for their flights at the end of the week. Truckers swung in from the highways. Early shifters picked up coffee and eggs on an English muffin, a yogurt parfait, a chocolate croissant, a cinnamon scone, or a blueberry muffin.

The wafting aromas of hot coffee and steamed buns evoked warm ambience contrasting with the pristine look of the café's clean shine. Spotless windows and sparkling table tops reflected early morning lights and shadows, natural and powered. Fall flowers in planters on the front terrace glistened with dew. The freshly hosed terrace slate walkways were as spick-and-span as a doorstep entry to a home in Holland. Out front, the café terrace tables were accented with brightly colored overhead umbrellas. The top of a cedar pergola floated high above, producing a balance of both light and shade throughout the popular open-air seating area.

The week had been normal, save for one elusive detail noted by the intern. Otherwise, matters were routine. The town was complacent. All was quiet on the central plains just west of Chicago and beyond the Illinois border. On the Mighty Mississippi, a tiny town balanced for dear life on the edge of the river bank on the Iowa side. So tiny it felt at times like it would plunge into the river below, sailing quietly away southward, traveling through the Delta and disappearing into the sparkling azure of the Caribbean Gulf.

Like the other lovely Iowa towns along the Western banks of the Mississippi River in Iowa, Sunnyside was an old town, river towns being the oldest in the state. Sunnyside liked to think of itself as a Wild West town. Really it was full of farmers and displaced city folk who wanted a decent place to raise their kids and get out of the rat race of the cities on the urban southern shores of the Great Lake Michigan. The farmers liked the soil on the prairie and the kinship in town, the small churches that dated back to the settlers, and the superior education in solid school systems - both public and private - with sports, fine arts, and new technology. For them, the normalcy was that they ran into the same people and had pretty much the same conversations every day at the same places in their town. The displaced city folk just wanted peace and quiet and the fact that they had figured out a way to escape urban crime and city streets, landing in the Sunnyside haven of sanity, serenity, and safety.

Jake and Stella Peltier, the coffee shop owners were no different. Their story of being high profile attorneys that left the big city for the small town, however, took a different twist in that they established their law practice with his and her law offices at the back of a coffee shop. Their two work quarters faced each other beyond the dining room. A hallway ran down the middle between them that led to the café back door. Stella had the south side office with south facing windows that brought in sunlight year-round and cool breezes when the weather was temperate and pleasant. Jake had the north office with windows looking out to the innards of the rest of the Wild

Mustang Corral, where they were located. The couple knew it would take time to establish their law practices as newcomer lawyers in a close-knit small town, so they came up with the idea to establish the coffee shop and put their legal services in the back, calling it, Legal Grounds Café.

To enhance their growth as a legal office and their place in the community as a café, Jake and Stella Peltier were active in the Sunnyside Chamber of Commerce. Often, the cafe hosted Chamber or church or club meetings. Because the café business was limited to breakfast, lunch, and after school, evenings were open for non-profits to use their space. Community was the name of the game for the two lawyers. It was why they came to Sunnyside from Chicago. Sunnyside was small and quaint yet business-rich. It was not backward. It was connected to the land, family friendly, promising-for-raising-children, and most of all, a highly polite and cultured society.

The coffee shop with the law offices meant there was some overlap of customers during the day, which was intentional and good for business. Folks came in, had coffee and got things done. Legal Grounds, with free wi-fi, was for working activities, or a place to stop on the way to engagements, or a place for a break on the way back from wherever they were coming from. For some patrons, such as the Twelve-steppers, it was a place to stop in for a cup of Joe, instead of sitting at a bar with a beer, before heading home. There were customers who scheduled their appointments at the café for signatures, sales, or new hires. They would sign papers with their realtor, converse with their broker, or just meet a new friend and then move on to do dinner with the new friend at Cowboy Jack's Supper Club, if the chemistry was right.

Sunnyside romantic dinners, partying in the evenings and late-night drinks occurred at Cowboy Jack's, which anchored the other end of the horseshoe-shaped Corral mall. This worked well for business and kept the Corral's eating establishments from competing. Cowboy Jack's was good for saloon lunches, supper club dinners, and live music with dancing into the night. Monday through Saturday, Jack's opened for lunch, barely, as they were the only one in the Corral with a bar for adult drinks. Then Jack's went all out for dinner with bands playing and couples swinging on the parquet floor, particularly on the weekends, into the wee hours. It was the place to be seen and it got a little rowdy at times. Jack's was where the action was in town. Most of the town gossip took place at Jack's amidst drinking, darts, dancing, dining, mixing, mingling, and a mish mash of social entanglements. It was a real live (as opposed to virtual) web. Proprietors Jack and Sara knew everybody, and at times, everybody's business, through no intention of their own.

Jack and Sara owned the Wild Mustang Corral and Jack thought of himself as a cowboy, his wife a cowgirl. Yes, they owned horses on their out-of-town hobby ranch, strictly for play. Their eldest daughter, Stella (Jake's wife), was now grown, educated and becoming established at Legal Grounds, in their very own Wild Mustang mall. Their youngest daughter, Madeira, was yet in graduate school. Now enjoying a couple of grandchildren, Jack and Sara were still solid as a couple and reliable as business people, well-loved and admired in Sunnyside. Jack and Sara were not religious, but they felt Sunday off was good for business and for family life.

For quieter family dinners, the Corral choice was a restaurant with a large central dining room and several banquet rooms, Sven and Wong's. They were located more toward the middle of the Corral mall. Dave Swenson and Lily Wong were a couple with now away-at-college kids. Sven and Wong offered Asian stir-fry with Scandinavian desserts for business lunches, family dinners, and weekend celebrations. The couple had combined standard Asian entrees and delicious Scandinavian desserts on their menu. They felt they had the best of both East and West to create a uniquely American cuisine. In addition, small plates included Asian savory baozi (meat-stuffed buns) and the opposite or Scandinavian sweet pastries. Western style sandwiches and Asian noodle soups were popular at lunch. Dinners included stir-fry and casseroles. However, the most popular way to experience Sven and Wong's was to order Asian stir-fry main courses family style, and end with the Scandinavian pies and pastries. Best of both. Yum.

Sven and Wong's Restaurant is where Jake and Stella as well as everyone else in the county, went for family birthdays, athletic team banquets, and church club gatherings. There was also take-out that was reasonable and delicious six days a week (closed on Mondays). The food was not truly Asian, and the desserts were not fancy French, however, for Sunnyside, Sven and Wong's provided a predictable destination for singles, couples, and families that didn't want to cook at home, and desired a quiet and peaceful lunch or dinner setting with friendly staff, but minus banter and fanfare. Minus alcohol, too.

In addition to the three restaurants, the Wild Mustang Corral had a sprinkling of small businesses in the semicircle. From the middle rose a singular tower, an office building with the Sunnyside Chamber of Commerce President occupying the penthouse or top floor of the six stories. The tower's other floors had various professional offices, and some spaces open for leasing and entrepreneurship.

Yes, the week had been normal at the Corral, save one hovering detail noted and eventually mentioned by the intern. On this particular Friday morning, manager Ellie, the lawyer owners' right hand in the café, had let herself and the intern in at 4:30 a.m. so they could open at 5 a.m. Once open, Ellie became occupied with the prep work for the day in their open kitchen behind the long serving counter at the front of the cafe. She also backed up Travis who ran the front counter and drive-through as barista. Travis kept an eye out for the steady coming and going of work-bound customers rushing in for their regular orders. In the traffic, Travis noted glamour appear and disappear. It was one of the Sunnyside High School Cheer Squad girls, rushing in the front door but slipping to the back offices in a desperate hurry. Quickly, she disappeared.

There was no real reason to observe this, but in an outpost where things are pretty much routine, Travis noticed. What made this Friday different, and the whole week different, was that each day at opening, a different lovely young lady from the Cheer Squad had slipped in and rushed to the back, but without a word.

By Friday, Travis knew the girls were going to see Stella, the lady lawyer owner. Usually, neither lawyer was in at five, when Ellie and Travis opened. On an ordinary day, Jake, the husband lawyer and partner, would show up at about eight for normal business hours. Stella would be getting their two children off to the local elementary school and come in even later. However, different this week, each day, Stella had entered quietly through the back door and gone into her back office for an appointment shortly after they opened, obviously having set a schedule with the Cheer Squad members ahead of time.

Why would five attractive and accomplished high school girls need lawyers? They had their whole lives ahead of them; it was obvious that they were not writing their wills. They were not ending marriages and needing divorce proceedings. They were not buying real estate with contracts to consider. They were not involved in a business. What kind of trouble or proceedings were their concern?

"Is anyone back there?" Travis turned around and asked Ellie as he poured another tall cup of coffee for a cabbie.

"Stella texted me to watch for her early client. I saw her car is parked at the back when I took out trash, so I assume she is in her office," Ellie assured the intern.

Travis raised his eyebrows with curiosity. So, what was coming down in Sunnyside and why would students be seeking an attorney? What was up at Sunnyside High School?

"Just checking," Travis replied and refilled the dark roast machine with grounds to run another batch of coffee. "This is day five with a fifth girl, Allison, running in to see Stella for an early morning appointment. Usually Jake shows up first for their clients while Stella gets their kids to school. And, as a rule, there is neither lawyer here for clients at the 5 a.m. opening."

Travis counted on his fingers, "Monday, it was Ashley. Tuesday, Claire. Wednesday, Megan showed up. Yesterday, I saw Emily rush back there, and now today, it's Allison. I know this group. They are all seniors, and they cheer for the football team. You'll see them at the game tonight, Ellie. Something is up," Travis commented.

"The legal stuff is none of our business," Ellie ended the conversation and focused on putting out pastries and sandwiches in the display case.

Both the intern Travis and the manager Ellie knew the legal affairs were none of their business, however, they observed this unusual legal crusade and wondered. They proceeded to think their own thoughts and keep it to themselves.

In truth, Ellie was also curious, and even more so than Travis. Ellie and her husband Bob had a daughter, their only child, at the high school. She made a brain note to check in later with her high school daughter about what was going on with the Cheer Squad and a lawyer - for five different girls - five star senior athletic and accomplished college preppies, the best of the best in the county. She decided to ask Cecile at home in the afternoon when her daughter returned from Robotics Club after school. Cecile was more techie than cheery, but in the small student body at Sunnyside, certainly she would know something. Her daughter might have the inside scoop of what was up with the Cheer Squad at Sunnyside High School – that required a lawyer.

Chapter Two
Art House Dinner

Friday, October 5th, 1 p.m., Ellie texted Bob: Hey, Love. Heading home. See you soon.

By 1 p.m., the Legal Grounds afternoon shift leader Parker and manager Ellie had completed the transition, so he could take over until closing at 5 p.m. Parker was a college student from the local community college, and like Travis, he was training in small business operations. It had not taken long for Ellie to do the hand-off to Parker, as he was a quick study, very punctual and hard-working. Fridays were not too busy in the afternoons since many in the town had weekend plans already in place that did not include the coffee shop. There would still be a ladies' group, the Garden of Prayer, that would convene over by the fireplace. However, there would not be too many students from the high school and college, studying and working on their laptops in the afternoon after classes. The students would be back to study later on the weekend.

Parker had arrived early, as usual, and had a quick after-class lunch before checking in for his shift at the point of sale or computerized system at the counter. The college students were paid well hourly and received credit for their training, however they carried benefits from their college. The part-time semi-retired dining room attendees had their retirement benefits, but Ellie was pleased that as the manager she carried full benefits for her whole family.

Ellie's husband, Bob, as a trucker running his own business, was thankful for this Monday through Friday daytime opportunity (school hours while their daughter, Cecile was still in high school) for his wife and family. The lawyers, Jake and Stella Peltier, had very high regard for Ellie. They trusted her completely and appreciated her professional management style in working with the interns, the baristas, the dining room staff, the contracted maintenance, and of course, the customers. It was a win-win working situation all around. Rather than build up a fortune, Jake and Stella wanted to maintain a staff from the community with relationships of trust while supporting each other. So far so good in the duration of the few short years Legal Grounds had been in operation.

Foremost on Ellie's mind that Friday afternoon was her question for her daughter, Cecile, about the Cheer Squad girls needing the consultation of a lawyer. Ellie drove home directly to the Art House warehouse property that she and Bob had converted to artist quarters and studios. When their daughter was born, and Ellie would no longer travel with truck driver Bob, they had borrowed money from their parents to purchase the abandoned warehouse just out of town. Then, they had worked with contractors to establish five useful floors for their family and for resident artist rentals. The first floor had a drive-through garage for Bob's semi, room for their family cars, a workshop for Bob, and a gallery space for the artists and their public events. The second-floor housed artist work studio rentals. The third and fourth floors were converted to apartment lofts for artist living quarters. The top floor, or their penthouse palace, was the residence for Bob and Ellie and their daughter Cecile. The roof had a private owner outdoor terrace and barbecue setting under the vast Iowa sky. For the artist colony, out back beside the parking lot, Bob had built a picnic and grilling area for all to use. In addition, since Ellie's art endeavor was pottery, a kiln was installed for the use of all resident potters. Ellie made sure this was established for their studio artists.

Most of the artists had their day jobs, but all were able to develop and practice their talent in a user-friendly setting. None were starving artists. The warehouse apartments and studios were well-designed, contemporary, affordable, and comfortable. The little community encouraged creativity, connections, and well-being. The gallery with an attached hostess kitchen on the first floor was an amenity included with their rentals, so they could produce shows onsite at will. Some of the artists preferred this to the travel and expense of art crawls, festivals, and traveling exhibitions. The colony was occupied at capacity most of the time. The draw was affordability as well as the converted warehouse amenities. The convenient location between Chicago, Des Moines, and the Quad Cities of Davenport and Bettendorf, Iowa, and Rock Island and Moline, Illinois, was also a plus.

Bob and Ellie felt that an affordable artists quarter was an important addition and would be an enduring asset to the Sunnyside community. They wanted to raise their daughter in a safe town like Sunnyside. However, they felt it need not be devoid of creativity and innovation. Ellie had always been a potter. Although, she had never been able to fully support herself with pottery, it was in throwing a pot that she maintained her inner sanctity. The warehouse first floor was also an amazing venue for Bob to garage and work on his truck. He could be inside doing maintenance even through the cold Iowa winters.

Together, Bob and Ellie Davis settled down and had their family – Cecile – in their ideal safe and inspired place,

Sunnyside. Surrounded by the artists of all kinds (painters, novelists, sculptors, playwrights and screenwriters, potters, musicians and composers, poets, carvers, etc.), Cecile had tried it all. Where her creative bent ended up surprised both Bob and Ellie. However, they went along with it. Cecile loved mechanics and robotics and had spent many a weekend afternoon with her dad in the garage. At this point, she had found her high school niche and was fully engaged in the Sunnyside High School Robotics Club. Cecile was headed for engineering as a career.

Now Ellie was fearful of what her daughter was dealing with among her classmates at school. It was exactly what Bob and Ellie had wanted to avoid, escape, and ignore by coming to Sunnyside and starting their Art House colony. As they raised Cecile, they had worked to create the colony and make it self-supporting. Once Cecile was in school, Ellie had worked a variety of jobs in nearby towns with benefits and regular hours. This latest one, managing at Legal Grounds for the lawyers, was the best job of all, with excellent pay, perfect hours, and generous benefits.

Bob and Ellie Davis had waited long enough to have children, so Bob didn't want to miss his daughter growing up. Like Jake and Stella Peltier with their law café, Bob Davis was one of a quarter of a million small business owners in Iowa. Thanks to the trucking business available in eastern Iowa, he was able to limit his work to runs from Chicago to Des Moines and throughout the river towns dotting both sides of the Mighty Mississippi on a daily basis. Bob was on the road Monday through Friday, mainly between the towns and industries. He would also take runs east and west, crisscrossing the tristate area of Iowa, Illinois (Chicago), and Nebraska (Omaha). He had enough deliveries in his independent trucking business to keep him busy and yet close to home almost on a nightly basis for dinner. Goodness, Cecile was already in high school, thinking about college, and oh my, how the time had flown!

Ellie had plenty of time to think about things as she went about straightening up the house from the early morning hours when they had all rushed out of the house to get off to school and work. She caught a glimpse of her own joyful smile in the mirror as she went through the hallway to throw in a load of laundry. This afternoon time between work and when everyone else arrived home was her moment of respite, catching up, and getting organized. After setting the washer, she made a cup of tea and took out a salad she had brought home from work.

As she finished her salad, Ellie reached across the breakfast bar for her iPad and set it beside her salad bowl. She looked up Steak de Burgo, a dish that she had become familiar with while traveling throughout Iowa with Bob. According to the recipe, the ingredients were on-hand (tenderloin steaks, butter, garlic, salt, pepper, fresh oregano, and fresh basil). White wine, heavy cream, and sautéed mushrooms were also suggested on some recipes. A baguette and a salad were shown as accompaniments in the pictures.

"Looks good," Ellie said to herself. After finishing her late lunch, Ellie emptied a packaged wild rice pilaf with spices in the rice cooker. Closer to dinner time, she would turn it on. This would be the other side dish with the Steak de Burgo.

Later in the afternoon, when Ellie was grilling the steaks, Cecile arrived home first, from school. After putting away her backpack and washing up, Cecile tossed a green salad and added chopped cucumber and carrots. A light vinaigrette tossed into the greens finished it. She went about setting their table for three and was just pouring ice water when her dad walked through the door.

Right at 5 p.m., Bob, Ellie, and Cecile were seated at their dining room table saying a prayer of thanks. They had a high school football game that began at 6 p.m., so they worked together to make dinner on time while enjoyable. The stadium was only five minutes away, so they had time to catch up on everyone's day before they left.

"How was your day?" Bob asked Cecile.

Cecile talked about a paper she was writing for English that was due on Monday – only the rough draft, though. Bob mentioned his run from Des Moines to the Quad Cities, where he had to wait while the dock staff unloaded. He was thankful they were efficient, so he was back on the road quickly and on time for dinner tonight.

"Great start to a wonderful weekend with two lovely ladies," Bob remarked, beaming.

Ellie commented about her day at Legal Grounds, and then she finally got around to bringing up her all-consuming big question. "What is going on with the Cheer Squad at Sunnyside High School where they would need a lawyer, of all things? I'm thinking a girl is in trouble, or the whole squad is in trouble," she probed Cecile as her voice drifted off.

Cecile wiped her mouth with her napkin, set it on her dinner plate, and then looked up. "Well, there's a girl they can't get in touch with, so the Cheer Squad is concerned."

"What?" asked Ellie. "Who is missing?" she added.

"No, Mom," Cecile corrected her mom. "We don't know if anyone is missing. Last year, Jade Johnson was the head of the Cheer Squad. She went off to college in Chicago, the University of Illinois, I think. Anyway, those girls are super-close. They've been in touch with her at the University and they've been to visit her Chicago apartment. Well, right now their friend Jade is not answering her phone – since last weekend. They don't understand why, and they are very concerned. So, the girls are probably asking the lawyers to help them locate their friend."

"What about Jade Johnson's parents – Joel and Cherise. Have the Cheer Squad girls contacted the parents with their questions and concern? Surely, they would be worried, or maybe they can inform the friends about what is happening with their daughter."

"Mom, that's a long story and I thought we were going to the game tonight," Cecile answered quietly.

"True, this can wait, I guess. Are you all right, Cecile?" asked Ellie.

"Mom, I'm fine," Cecile reassured her mom. "It's a very nice group of girls – the Cheer Squad – but it's not really my group. They care about their friend at the University, but maybe she just changed her cell phone number or lost her phone. Maybe it's a connectivity issue. Hopefully, everything is fine."

There was a pause.

"Mom, my friends are waiting in the bleachers at the game," Cecile interrupted the silence.

"Dearest Cecile, you can go along now and meet your friends. Dad and I will be sitting in our usual spot up top, under the announcer's broadcast box. We'll be there shortly after we load these dishes. Just leave everything as it is. Be sure there's gas in your car and take a hoodie. Chilly night. Love you," Ellie replied.

With farewells, Cecile was out the door and down the stairs to her car in the garage. Ellie and Bob listened for a moment, attuned to sounds that carried up the private open stairwell. They heard the automatic garage door open, Cecile's car exit, and then waited for the door to return back down.

Ellie looked at Bob (who was a little puzzled) as they loaded the dishwasher, then spoke up, "I had hoped to mention the Cheer Squad even before dinner to get the drift of what is going on at the high school. We didn't really have time for an in-depth face-to-face. I had wanted to connect with Cecile about her high school classmates who seem to be showing up in spades to see the lawyers in the back room, at the crack of dawn, at Legal Grounds. All week, the lady lawyer has been there for them, when usually it is Jake who opens the law office in the morning and Stella, his wife, comes in later. A change in routine, any slight change is so notable in this small town, Bob. I need to know what is going on. This is our daughter's high school. We're talking about sweet, beautiful, highly accomplished young ladies."

"I can see that it's a concern, Dear," Bob responded.

"We want to raise our daughter in a safe environment. At least we are talking about Chicago, apparently, in regard to this girl that is missing. I mean, it is nothing that is going on in our community, I guess. Jade Johnson could have enrolled at the community college close by instead of landing all the way in urban Chicago right out of high school," Ellie noted.

"I don't know about life at the universities, but with girls out in the world and away from home, things can happen, sometimes bad things," Bob commented.

"What are you thinking, Bob?" Ellie asked.

"I'm thinking about something we learned at a trucker conference a while back. There's a sharp midwestern agent, a woman from a few states over, Oklahoma to be exact, whose work is sometimes present at the conferences. Almost a decade ago, she noticed a pattern. There had been a fair number of missing persons and bodies dumped along the major highways in this country. Terri Turner is her name and she's a Supervisory Intelligence Analyst with the Oklahoma Bureau of Investigation.

As Ellie's mouth dropped to the floor, Bob continued, "What Turner found was that though most truckers are hard-working and decent, there are a few that use their occupation to victimize people who are stranded, or are hitchhikers, but mainly that are prostitutes that hang out at the truck stops. A number of former drivers have committed atrocious crimes and are now on death row as serial killers. They used our highways as their hunting and dumping ground. Eventually, the FBI caught on with the *Highway Serial Killings Initiative.* They focused on killers who choose their victims and abandon their bodies along highways. The findings began about a decade ago."

"Bob, that's terrifying. This Sunnyside girl does not hang out at truck stops. She went off to a university to get a degree," Ellie proclaimed.

"Ellie, I know. And I don't know anything about the University of Illinois in Chicago. I only know that in my own profession, there are bad people that do bad things. I've followed the story since the FBI would like us to keep our eyes out for innocent people being victimized on our highways. About five years ago, a journalist named Ginger Strand wrote a story in *This Land Press,* covering Ms. Turner's work. It's a cold cruel world out there sometimes," Bob explained.

"Do campus girls go missing? One would think Jade would know to stay away from risky and hazardous situations – but then we shouldn't blame the victim, either. We don't even know what happened to her. Let's hope for the best, and that the lawyers AND the Johnsons can figure out what happened to our hometown girl who went away to college," Ellie stated.

And Bob and Ellie left for the game.

Chapter Three
The Perfect Place

Friday, October 5th, 6 p.m., Bob drove, Ellie texted Cecile: 5 minutes. Want a hotdog?

Since they had missed the kick-off anyway, Bob stopped at the concessions stand and sent Ellie on her way, up to their bleacher seats just below the announcer box. Their usual crowd of other couples was already seated and munching on nachos while sipping on soft drinks. Ellie put a blanket down on the bleachers for Bob and herself, and then glanced around. She spotted her daughter right away, sitting among her Robotics Club friends down front near the 50-yard line. They looked like they were having a grand old time on a Friday night together, laughing and carrying on.

Cecile hadn't wanted anything from the refreshments stand so Bob soon returned with just two hot herbal teas for the two of them. They could bring a thermos, they knew, but they wanted to support the Booster Club with sales. Friday night football was the perfect place for Ellie to reassure herself that her little town of Sunnyside, Iowa, where she and Bob had chosen to settle down and raise their lovely daughter Cecile, was the perfect decision. Indeed, they had landed in the perfect place was her observation on this brisk fall evening. The high school was college preparatory but fun and practiced the joy of learning. Community was important, social life was encouraged, and relationships were valued. On Fridays, pretty much everyone in Sunnyside showed up at the Sunnyside High School Stadium for the game, wholesome, friendly, and enjoying each other's company.

Down below them, Ellie noticed attorney Jake Peltier at his usual spot at the game with his children, Ben and Emma. An engaged dad, he had the kids for outings and activities on Friday nights while his wife Stella attended Bonfire Books, her club activity, going on at the café after hours.

"How are things at Legal Grounds, Ellie?" asked Carol nearby.

"Things are well. I love it there, Carol. Jake and Stella are terrific employers," Ellie answered.

"Yes, Jake seems like a community leader. Isn't he part of the Chamber of Commerce?" Carol asked.

"Very active," Ellie responded. "It's quite remarkable, being from back East and new to the Midwest, you know. He grew up in Maine. Eventually, he first came to Chicago where he and Stella worked together for Big Law. It was those two darling little children that they have that brought Stella back to her hometown, with Jake her Eastern husband. He likes it here, though."

"I heard he has a boat down at the Mississippi Marina," Carol mused.

"Jake is a boat guy. He brings his love for the water and boats all the way from Portland, Maine. Good match – here on the Mighty Mississippi in Sunnyside, Iowa. Perfect place in the Midwest for a boat lover from back East."

At halftime, the marching band came on the field while the players convened in the locker rooms with their coaching staffs. The game was tied, the air was crisp, and the bleacher chatter continued.

"Did you hear about the bill regarding Friday night football introduced last year by Iowa Republican State Representative Peter Cownie, of West Des Moines?" Caleb asked Bob.

"Why would we need a bill about Friday night football? We're all here," Bob replied.

"Well, apparently, that's the issue. The Big Ten introduced broadcasting collegiate games on Friday night – like on Fox, ESPN, you know, network television," Caleb went on.

"That doesn't make sense," Bob noted as others grunted with him. "Like I said, we are all here."

"Friday night is high school football's night, today, traditionally, and forever," someone added. "Just as sure as Wednesday is church night, Friday is football. We don't need some network folk interfering with our hometown Friday football nights. It's a town event."

"Tell that to the Networks. At least that guy from West Des Moines gets it. Some city folks get it," Caleb stated. "The point is, don't pit the Hawkeyes games against the hometown high school games. They should have the collegiate events during the rest of the weekend, but please leave Friday for high school teams."

When the teams came back on the field, all attention turned back to the game.

Carol and Ellie watched the Cheer Squad take the sidelines and perform their cheers.

"Were you a cheerleader in high school, Ellie?" Carol asked.

"No, not part of that crowd, Dearie. How about you?" Ellie returned the question.

"I went to a private high school and we didn't have a cheering squad," admitted Carol.

"Do you think you missed something, Carol?" asked Ellie.

"No, I didn't miss it. We went to the Friday night games and all, but as girls we were also busy with other sports – like gymnastics and dance. So, I didn't miss it," Carol recalled. "Sometimes we performed at halftime. That was fun, although it could get cold out there on the field in a costume – even when we were moving around quite a bit. Iowa weather is not for the timid, I say."

"Well, our Cheer Squad here at Sunnyside looks like they are very athletic, and I heard that they must carry an above-average GPA to be on the Squad," Ellie noted.

"Oh, I am sure they are all college-bound," remarked Carol. "If kids are smart nowadays, they pursue higher education, something beyond high school anyway. Everyone loves a small town, but everyone wants greater opportunities in life, too."

"You are absolutely right on that one. Sunnyside High School has so many avenues to begin on the path to future goals. Our dear little Cecile is down front with her Robotics Team friends.

It will be engineering for her someday, I'm sure," added Ellie with a pleasant and joyous smile.

As the sun had set and the stadium lights were in full radiance, the friends continued their visit while their beloved home team lost. It was all fine, though. They were together and happy to be there as a community on a Friday night, celebrating youth, education, and generations of each other, those coming up into high school, and those who had long since moved on and established their lives.

For Ellie, it was the perfect place and they all had each other.

Chapter Four
Bonfire Books Reads *Out from the Jaws of the Dragon 1: The Pastor*

Friday, October 5th, 6 p.m., Stella texted Louisa Moore: Leaving. Start without me.

On Friday night while Jake was at the football game with the children and most of the folk of the Sunnyside area, Stella was going to Legal Grounds to attend the community book club called Bonfire Books. A senior couple in town, Jerry and Louisa Moore, had started the Bonfire group a decade ago, as they entered retirement. Each month, the group savored a new book together, with chapters assigned for the Friday night weekly discussion. Jake and Stella were keen to this group using their business space on a weekend night. Usually, Stella attended the club while Jake took the children out on the town for a special night with Dad. After the club meeting and the children's outing, Stella and Jake put their tired children to bed, and then debriefed with a bottle of wine and quality couple time together at the end of their work week. Friday perfect.

Bonfire Books had varied interests. Sometimes the group partnered with Out With Owen & Willow: O WOW! Travel and did global excursions to coincide with a book. *The Sweet Life in Paris* by David Lebovitz precluded a grand tour of the cuisine and art of the City of Lights. For *In the Garden of Beasts* by Erik Larsen the group spent ten days in Berlin. *Spring Moon* by Bette Bao Lord brought the group to China, back in time and forward, wandering in the transformed cities of Xi'an and Shanghai.

This month, the club was reading a novella, first of a series, with the fictional story of a young person's success in facing challenge, *Out from the Jaws of the Dragon,* by Taylor O'Brien. Some of the book club members had crossed paths with similar narratives over the years in their professions (school counselors, health workers, educators). The group read three chapters each week and then discussed O'Brien's work of fiction. O'Brien's tale featured a character named Sophia Lewis, who came out from the jaws of a dragon to land in the hands of her Creator God. In the novella's storyline she brings to light her journey and shares insights of overcoming challenges. Throughout the series, the protagonist leverages ten tools for success: a good education, wonderful friends, reading the Bible with prayer, healthy relationships, developing her skills, travel, establishing herself as a professional, a supportive marriage, raising her own lovely children, and the Lord Jesus Christ as her Shepherd.

As a book club, the readers felt this fictional story was a way of understanding more about what was being revealed in the news media about what can happen to children, and how to be supportive. They were raising awareness of resolve in getting out, moving on, and succeeding in life. Although no two stories would be exactly alike, the club saw this as a case study. It was a coming-of-age story or Bildungsroman that was, in essence, a modern-day Charles Dickens fable. As they read, they also felt free to talk about their own stories. They were seeking to connect with God, be in touch with themselves, listen to others, and understand society. "Love one another, as Jesus loves you," was their theme for the month.

The fictional saga began with the main character, Sophia, as an established adult, reflecting on her little girl childhood, in the safe presence of the Lord Jesus Christ as her Shepherd. O'Brien wrote that Sophia used journaling to reflect and to fellowship with her God about her victory over her childhood experiences and memories, people and places. Bonfire Books began by discussing what they had read in the opening or part one of the novella.

* * *

Out from the Jaws of the Dragon, Part 1: The Pastor
In the early hours of a morning, the Shepherd would lead a girl - out of a married professional woman in bed with her husband. Stepping softly in the dim light of the hallway, the Shepherd and the girl were careful not to awaken the woman's children. Pausing at the nursery the girl studied their innocent sleeping faces. Her heartbeat synchronized with their breathing. She inhaled the children's peacefulness and her tiny inner being was flooded with a white light. God made them, innocent, and now God's Son, the Shepherd, held her hand. She felt hope for rebirth.

Passing the bathroom, a mirror reflected the little girl's pastel dress with puffy sleeves, white lace, and a satin sash tied in a bow at the back. It was a dress just like the Shepherd would have wanted for her. In the dining room, the child turned on the chandelier and climbed up onto a chair at the table. Dangling her legs, she crossed her feet, white anklets with lace and white sandals. The girl's long auburn hair flowed across her shoulders and onto the table like heavy embroidered silk.

The Shepherd's hand rested on the girl's shoulder. His presence warmed her heart. His words were in her thoughts, "I am the way, the truth, and the life; no one comes to the Father, but by me."

Sophia was seeking the confidence that God cares. She wanted to look to her Heavenly Father and confide her soul's deepest longings, just as the Psalmist wrote in Psalm 62, "My soul finds rest in God alone, for my salvation comes from him." Sophia wanted to know that God was different, that is, trustworthy. She wanted to know that he does not force, does not shame, does not control, and does not intimidate. She pursued the one who asks, who respects agency, who does not demand, who does not expect a reward. No payback solicited.

The Shepherd would visit when the woman was sleeping, taking the hand of the child, and leading her to the table to write. The girl followed him, believing the truth would set her free. She poured out hidden pictures from her past, spilling them onto white paper. By day, the girl was afraid because no one would believe her. As a professional adult woman, Sophia was especially calculated and exact, wanting documented facts - only what was acceptable to the authorities she knew. There would be no fantasy, no malingering, and no pity. Life would go on in an orderly fashion with tranquility, intelligence, truth, and honor. The woman reminded the girl of when she had tried to tell before, how she was ordered to keep quiet, to hide with all of her pain. The words had been difficult to find; the girl did not understand what had happened. There was confusion, embarrassment, and shame.

Because no one would speak to the girl and no one would listen, she did not talk; she smiled but had no voice. The girl had come to understanding through books, so she did not know spoken words, only written words. It was in a book that she had met the Shepherd. God's book spoke to her; now she would speak to the page.

The message came out, painful unsaid secrets released to the blank page. The little girl wrote down her experience, not to achieve, but to unravel the truth before the listening ear of the Shepherd and to find strength to prevail over what she had experienced.

The little girl's life would unfold in the heart of the Shepherd.

The girl self of Sophia wanted to feel safe with the Shepherd and she wanted to trust him with her pain. The girl wanted to love him, get close to him, and whisper into his ear her story. The little girl wanted to cry on his shoulder; she wanted to feel his love and care while resting in his arms. It was the safe blank page through which the child and the Shepherd conversed. The girl wrote. The Shepherd listened, and when he spoke, his words responded with the wisdom, truth, and honor that would set her free.

Sophia began with writing about a summer day at church camp when she was in middle school.

On a calm and beautiful afternoon, a soft breeze flickered silvery leaves, reflecting the sun. Overlooking a glassy still lake, two rickety folding chairs hung on a rocky cliff outside a camp dining hall. Lunch dishes were heard clattering from behind the windows.

A young camper, Sophia, had gone up to the administration building to meet the camp pastor. At age thirteen, Sophia had never before confided with a church leader. Together they walked down the hillside on a narrow trail, through the trees, past a noisy soccer field, muddying up their shoes. Drifting scents of the pines above and the smell of the clay path below held the two beings suspended between earth and sky. The gentleman had ducked inside the hall, grabbed two chairs, and set them on the cliff. Jutting out from the trees, it was as though they were going to fall off the edge of the world and into the lake below.

The pastor was massive and filled up all the space, like a god, towering over the girl, blocking the sun. His dark hair was creamed back from a forehead that stretched up into the heavens. His face wore full lips that flapped as he talked, pillars of white teeth, perfectly tanned smooth skin, and steely blue eyes without expression. The churchman was clean, with no evident touch of the world. She wondered if he would be able to understand from his clean world, if he could help. Reassuring herself, the girl felt very positive. Yes, Sophia thought, as a pastor, he would like her to learn to be clean. It was God who called men to be pastors. This man was sent by God, she reasoned. The pastor liked to speak God's Word. Sophia trusted him. She felt the pastor would speak God's Word to her.

Sophia angled her leg around a leg of the cold metal folding chair, attempting words, her heart pounding from her chest. She had to speak; it was she who had requested the meeting. Yet Sophia felt that if she opened her mouth, she would vomit. With sweaty hands, Sophia wrung her front shirttail into a knot. Her face flushed red with embarrassment and pain. She was almost a young woman, confessing hatred of her father. At last she found the words to say it, but they seemed to tell too much too fast. It hurt to hold the truth in; it hurt to let it out. The Bible said to speak the truth in love, but at the same time, no unwholesome word was to be spoken. Sophia felt confused and compelled. She wanted to clean out her insides. She yearned for God and his purity.

Warm midsummer wind blew through their conversation, sweeping a shiny lock onto the pastor's face. He swept it back with a quick motion of his hand. Folded quietly on his knee, his hands rested while Sophia spoke from an anguishing heart. The pastor's hands were large hands but, unlike her father's large pale hands, his were tanned and medical doctor sterile. She noticed that the pastor's hands did not threatened to touch her; they suggested running away and shunning her if she were not clean also.

Sophia looked down and ran her fingers across her new pastel jeans, and then noted her spotless matching flower-patterned shirt. She felt her shiny clean reddish hair feathering in the wind. If only she could be clean inside and free from the father hatred. If only she could cross the line into the world of good people. Maybe, then, God would love her, too.

The pastor addressed her, "my friend," in a tempered voice, unrelated to his resounding preaching at the chapel the night before. Sophia wanted to be his friend. He had preached respect for parents, the fifth commandment, to a camp full of indifferent middle school students. Standing over them, arms outstretched, his words reverberating throughout the chapel, he had thrust his head forward in staccato rhythm, thundering, "Exodus 20, verse 12 says, 'Honor your father and your mother: that your days may be long in the land which the Lord your God gives you.' Obey them, and then tell them you love them. God has sent his Son to die for you, granting you his love and forgiveness. Can you not obey and love your parents?

If you turn from them, you are likewise turning from God and his love."

How Sophia wanted to be God's friend, but in her heart, she found a knot of hatred and fear. Prayer and confession did not remove it, nor did tears, denial, or determination. Sophia knew she hated her dad, but she did not understand why.

Sophia's dad seemed like a regular guy, just like everyone else's dad, maybe even better. Doug Lewis was a leader in the church and their suburban community. He assisted in the youth program and attended the Spring Meadow Council meetings. He had provided for his family an elegant Tudor-styled home in a wholesome neighborhood with an excellent school district. People thought of Doug as friendly and kind, a Good Samaritan who would step up and help anyone in need. Socially at ease, Doug would joke and laugh amiably, especially with women, and with younger women in particular (who sometimes called him, "Dapper D"). A typical dad - admired, accepted and loved by all.

There were things about him that felt strange, particularly to a teenager, but these did not seem unusual. He hated contemporary music with a passion and confiscated his children's iPods if he heard them playing anything other than traditional religious hymns. Adamantly against most movies, he viewed Hollywood as a city of sin. The Lewis children were directed to choose friends mainly in the church, and Doug criticized schools and government as invasive. In many ways, the Lewis children felt their dad was overzealous and outdated, but it did not feel right to hate him. All dads seemed old-fashioned to their teenaged children. Moreover, as the pastor had quoted the Bible, children were to love and obey their parents, no matter how old-school they seemed.

After the chapel service, Sophia had gone to bed in turmoil. Her hatred caused great anxiety and heaviness, and the pastor's words stuck to her insides. In her desire for God's love, she could pretend to accept her father like everyone else, but in sleep, buried secrets surfaced in recurring dreams.

The nightmare came in the dark of the night, extortionist, and robber of tranquility. She slept. She awoke. She was dreaming. She fought with her father's hands in her pajamas. His large, thick palm held her, fingers toying with her, as he lay parallel to her, pressed tightly against her body. His lips swallowed her lips; his tongue filled her mouth. Her struggles to get away were met with several hundred pounds of force. When she grabbed at his wrist to pull his hands away, nothing happened. He was cemented in place.

Sophia turned off her body, refusing to participate. Her mind pretended he was not in her bed. She lay powerless, willing herself to forget in the moment it happened. Even during nights when she was left alone, she was terrorized, feeling him touching her again and again. Pretending had not succeeded. Helplessness and nakedness invaded her sleep. Present or not, Dapper D haunted the night.

At camp, Sophia's recurring nightmare surfaced and then ended in a hellish vision of flames surrounding her in bed. She was being consumed by a burning hatred, with no escape from her father or from her guilt.

Away from home, where her father could not appear, Sophia felt that for the first time she connected her hatred with the trauma of being forced to sleep with her dad. She began to associate her fear and anxiety with his visits to her bed at night. She thought perhaps if she were not afraid, there would be no hatred. She wanted to love her dad, and she wanted to obey God. It occurred to her at camp that the man of God, the pastor, would have a solution. The pastor seemed informed about parents, children, feelings, and God. He spoke with authority.

The next morning, Sophia asked to talk with the pastor.

They sat by the lake.

"Did he rape you?"

"He touches me all over."

"Did he molest you?"

"Maybe, he sleeps in my bed with me."

Unsure of the details of rape and having never before heard the word "molest", Sophia did not know how to respond. She tried to explain her hatred and fear. She tried to communicate how she felt she could not love her dad.

The conversation was brief. The clergyman said he needed to consider the matter, and asked to meet again the following day, same time and place. He requested that Sophia bring her Bible to the meeting the next day.

Chapter Five
Bonfire and *Out from the Jaws of the Dragon 2: The Pastor's Answer*

(Bonfire Books moved on to discuss the second part of their selected novella, where the main character, Sophia, considers what she thought was her normal Christian family and her wonderful church pastor.)

Sophia arose with peace and confidence in her God and in her pastor. She had done what God desires: she had told the truth. She had trusted. Faith and hope raced through her mind and emotions. She sighed with a great relief.

The pastor was a respected church leader, almost worshiped in the community and in the Lewis home. On Sundays, Doug Lewis recorded the pastor's sermons and then played them over during the week as if this were the ONLY pastor in the world, a true authority from God.

The Lewis clan was a churched family. They attended services regularly and they had many friends in the church. The Lewis estate was a bed-and-breakfast for church friends and their families when they passed through for religious conventions. The Lewis family, in turn, frequented their out-of-town Christian friends' homes for holidays.

Mrs. Doug Lewis, Bethany, loved entertaining. She decorated the house and planned menus weeks in advance of the visits. Her cooking for these events had flair with gourmet quality: entrees such as steamed fresh lobster, or herbed roast pork loin. Before the meal, Beth served shrimp cocktail and canapés, but no wine or martinis (strictly forbidden among the faithful). The table, with carefully pressed linens and center-pieced with fresh flowers from her garden, was laden with many courses, and garnished with homemade jellies and pickles. For dessert, there were rich mousses or home-churned ices.

After meals, from the dining room, the women moved into the kitchen for dishes, the men to the sitting room for conversation, and the children raced to the neighborhood playground for a soccer game.

When Sophia, her siblings, and the visiting children came in from outside, they would find their parents reunited in the kitchen, around the enormous gothic oak table, teapot on, close to pastries and sandwiches. Late into the night, the grown-ups would discuss politics, theology, and society, quoting the Bible and the newspapers, the women affirming the opinions of the men, pausing only to sip sweet tea or drink robust creamed coffee and circulate nourishment.

"Beth, how fortunate to have a husband who speaks with Biblical authority," someone would comment, and Beth would turn to look deep into the eyes of Doug and nod, her face glowing with pride.

The Lewis children savored freedom when their parents entertained. Secretly they huddled with their friends around a computer, playing video games and listening to popular music with the other church children (games and music not forbidden in their homes). However, when the Lewis children were caught in disobedience, Doug's temper flared in the presence of everyone. When his children were small, Doug would strip them from the waist down and beat them in front of the approving guests.

"He that spares the rod, hates his children, but he that loves his children, chastens them early," Doug would declare with assurance.

The Lewis children assumed that their dad knew best, that they were unusually bad, and that this kind of treatment was necessary even though they never saw it required for other children. The visiting adults would praise Doug's control of the situation. Bethany would again look into his eyes with approval and pride. A sort of relief would settle into the air. Doug was taking care of things by keeping evil out of his family. All could rest and feel secure. Doug radiated with pride and respect; sin was not going to flourish in his home.

As the Lewis children became teenagers, Doug grew more reserved in his exhibition of control at times when guests were present. However, in the private lives of the Lewis home, Doug gradually exercised comprehensive governance and established new rules to deal with his perception of adolescent sin. His children were forbidden from dressing in private. They were not allowed to close their bedroom doors or the bathroom door. Doug would confiscate their music, games, electronics, and books. Their time away from home became strictly limited, and at home, Doug demanded greater attention, allegiance, and affection. The children understood that it was only their dad's presence and his power that protected them from their sins.

Even though Sophia generally was the focus of many of these punishments, (an understood necessity if her glimmer of agency was to be subdued), the church held a special kind of magic for her. Sophia believed in God and in His community, the church. She saw the church leaders as men who loved and represented God. She desired to behave and to belong to God's kingdom even though she felt she was bad. Sophia searched for goodness, and longed to offer herself, cleansed and chaste, to the service of God.

When the camp pastor and Sophia met for the second time, the next day, her heart was pounding with willingness and inner zeal.

The verse the pastor shared was I John 1: 9: "If we confess our sins, he is faithful and just to forgive us our sins, and to cleanse us from all unrighteousness."

As they looked at the verse in Sophia's Sunday School Bible, the pastor pulled out a blue pen from his white shirt pocket and wrote in the margin, "Joyful Trails Christian Camp".

He turned his gaze and regarded Sophia saying, "Sophia, if you confess your sin of hating your father, God will forgive you. God promises to take away that hatred right now. These verses were written directly for you," and he crossed out the pronouns as they occurred in print, replacing them with her name.

"If Sophia confesses her sins, he is faithful and just to forgive Sophia her sins, and to cleanse Sophia from all unrighteousness."

"But what if my dad does it again and I hate him again?" Sophia asked with a puzzled look on her face and a twisting in her stomach.

"You can stay at a friend's house if you like," was the pastor's reply.

Friends. Doug did not allow his children to associate closely
with anyone. Moreover, there was no "if you like" in the Lewis
household - except what Doug liked, as specified by the
teachings of the church. Moreover, Sophia felt that the young
people she knew at church would never come to her rescue
when it came to her dad. She could not invite herself over to
their homes against her father's wishes. She had no experience
with church friends being there when she needed them. If the
pastor could not help her, how would the church people be able
to assist?

Sophia noticed that the man of God was no longer looking at
her. He was no longer listening. She searched for and found his
eyes empty and blank. His mind was set on what he had to say.

"But you must have friends. Now one more thing," the pastor
continued. "You must promise me never to tell anyone about
this, especially your mother. If you do, you will be responsible
for dividing your parents' marriage and God hates that. God
hates divorce, and you will cause their divorce. You would not
want to be responsible for that too, would you?"

Sophia's countenance sank into her lap, melting with shame
and guilt. She nodded. A lump came up in her throat as she
held back hot tears of disappointment and dread.

"Your dad is a very insecure and sensitive man who needs you.
He is important to our community and he gives a lot to our
church. When I see him at youth group, leading the young
people, I don't know what we would do without his
contribution and leadership. Doug needs the confidence that his
sweet little girl can give him. Therefore, when you get off the
bus from camp, run up to your father, throw your arms around

him, and tell him how much you love him. He deserves your affection and love. Embrace him with all you've got. He and your mother are having problems right how; it is your duty to help. Be supportive of your dad. Make him feel wanted, appreciated, and in charge. Stand in the gap for this godly man, child, as it is the least you can do for all you've been given."

Silence. Fear. Sophia wondered, "How?" She was terrified.

The pastor went on, "I can see you are not starving, young lady, are you? You should be thankful for the food and shelter your dad provides for you. Now show your dad appreciation and make him feel good. There are people all over the world who are much worse off than you. Furthermore, those who live in hatred are likened unto murderers in the Bible, 'Whosoever hates his brother is a murderer, and you know that no murderer has eternal life abiding in him.' It sounds like you have murdered your father many times over, my friend. Now let's pray and confess your sins so God can forgive you."

The Bible verse pricked Sophia's concerns and suddenly she felt that if she didn't readily accept what the pastor said, she would drown in evil. Her hesitations were quickly submerged as she bowed her head under the umbrella of the leader's stature, and prayed,

"Dear God, I want to love you and I want to love my dad. I want to be a good Christian girl. I confess to you my hatred and thank you for your forgiveness as you have promised in your Word. Thank you for my pastor who has heard my prayer and guided me into light. Amen."

The church leader, impatient, rushed to complete the prayer, "Lord Jesus, receive this young woman into your kingdom today, by the power of your forgiveness. She has confessed the hardness of her heart. I thank you she has been willing to come forward, admit her guilt, and receive your blessing. Give her compassion for her dad, great man of faith that he is. We praise you that she has a wonderful Christian dad who loves her and cares for her. May she love, honor, and obey her parents all the days of her life. Bless her father, Doug, in his walk with you, and as the spiritual leader of his household. In your holy name, we pray. Amen."

As they prayed, Sophia did feel forgiven. Secretly she prayed that she would be able to hug her dad and be brave enough to be affectionate with him. If the pastor said this would solve the Lewis family problems, Sophia felt she had to try it. There was too much unhappiness to risk not doing what the pastor said. This was her chance, Sophia felt. Her only hope. It was the pastor's advice and he made it sound like an easy thing to do.

Take care of your dad. Take care of the marriage of your mother and father. Don't tell anyone. Throw your arms around him. Sophia had her spiritual instruction from her spiritual leader.

It is said that when you drown, you remember your whole life. On the bus ride home from camp, Sophia drowned, experiencing feelings from memories that were never discussed. At the same time, she tried to imagine herself running up and hugging her dad.

As the camp bus pulled into the church parking lot, and awaiting cars came into view, campers were yelling out of the windows and parents were running up to the bus. Sophia wrestled inside. Doug Lewis, late as usual, was not around. In anticipation of his arrival, she thought of the church leader's words. Her insides begged her, "No!" She did not feel safe, as she had hoped she would after talking with the pastor. She felt responsible.

The Lewis family minivan finally screeched to a quick stop in front of a now empty church lawn. As her dad hopped out of the car and came toward her, Sophia's heartbeat raced in double time to his every step. His approach took forever.

"How was camp, Sophie?" he asked.

Sophia slowly answered as she assisted with her bags, "I love you, Dad." She had said the words. Inside, she felt, "I want to love you, Dad, I really want to. But I am afraid."

Chapter Six
Bonfire and *Out from the Jaws of the Dragon 3: Good Little Girl*

(Bonfire Books concluded this Friday with their newly selected novella by going over the third part of the reading. Here, the main character, Sophia, reviews what she remembers from birth and as a small child.)

In the beginning there was silence: deafening, intangible stillness, immobility, black and cold. Silence was Sophia's refuge from birth. Her crying was never answered by her mother. The womb that spit her out on dry land hadn't wanted her. She did not understand but she learned to be silent and still.

Crying meant she was handed over to her father. She could taste him, smell him, and feel him, already taking over her body and her being, from the beginning when he heard her infant cries for her mother. Mrs. Lewis had Mark and Molly, her twins, her beloveds. It was Mr. Lewis who walked the floor nightly to calm Sophia and she would pay him back, he decided. The deal was struck at birth. She was his. Bethany was preoccupied with her perfectly precious twins. God gave Doug little Sophia all for himself.

There were voices around her. She was silent until she had to talk, and yes, she was made to talk, to respond, as they wanted. She grew a voice, their voice, what they wanted to hear. She learned when she was supposed to speak because silence at the wrong time was punishable. She would say what she had to, and her words were theirs. She learned to sing and perform, recite stories and poetry. She learned how to participate. Inside silence reigned, the inner her that never cried, never needed, never wanted. Inside, the girl was forever silent.

When they were very young, their family usually visited friends on Sunday afternoons. On the ride home, Mr. and Mrs. Lewis would argue. Frightened of the yelling, Sophia tried to ignore them, until her father, making no headway with her mother, would blast her for being a bad girl on the visit. Mark would chime in "Sophie whines until she gets what she wants."

Mr. Lewis would continue, "When are you going to learn how to behave, Sophie?"

Silence. Shame. She stared at the trees floating by the car window, on the boulevard - the space separating home and other.

Mrs. Lewis proclaimed, "Mark and Molly have always been tender, shy and sensitive. They return our love. Sophia, it's too bad you don't appreciate anything."

The trees rolling past in the dark serenely inhaled the hurtful words on her behalf - until they drove up the driveway. When the car engine halted, she felt like throwing up, like bursting, or exploding a bomb so nothing would be left of her, her black ashes disappearing into the black asphalt driveway.

Suddenly, her insides did explode in sobs on the lawn. Her body slammed to the ground, arms flailing, fists pounding the grass, kicking and screaming, tears bleeding into the earth. She wanted to be good - she could not control herself she wanted them to love her, too. Why couldn't she behave? She didn't mean to disappoint them so. She wanted to be like Mark and Molly.

"Why does she carry on so - this brat? I guess she's spoiled rotten, that's why," Mrs. Lewis complained with exasperation and disgust.

"I'll give her something to cry about. Little Sophie, I'll give you something to cry about," Mr. Lewis threatened in reply. His huge arm plucked the body up off the grass, his hand dangling it high into the air by its hair. With glazed eyes, a frowned brow, mouth smirking, and tightly clenched teeth, his face was a knot of taut emotion. He tore off the clothes and beat a bare bottom with massive slaps of his palm. If it was still daylight, neighborhood children would gather to watch the man beat the naked girl.

I can hold back, she would tell herself. She knew how, overcoming all feeling, control took over, so she could face home.

"There, that will teach you," Mr. Lewis said. But it didn't. Again, and again the man would beat the little girl.

On another day, one hot summer afternoon, Sophia rode her tricycle on the sidewalk in front of the stately Lewis Tudor home. Sophia ventured to join Mark and Molly among the neighborhood gang down the block. When she reached the group, the older children surrounded her tricycle, smiling. An older boy, nine or ten, stepped forward and glared into her eyes. At three or four, she felt small before him. Her auburn hair, braided neatly, rested on her shoulders.

Her outfit, a printed cotton top, matching shorts with an elastic waist, white sandals with white anklets, felt clean and fresh. She held on to her tricycle looking up at him, not daring to move. Sunlight beamed through the trees and reflected off the chrome of the handlebars. She squinted. He reached over to the pink elastic waistband on her shorts, pulled them open, along with the underpants, and looked down. As he held them open, the group drew closer and looked inside. He began to describe aloud what he saw.

"Hey, look what I see, guys, a real pussy. How about a little pussy, guys?"

Sophia froze. Deaf, mute, paralyzed. Her insides were falling, plunging in space with nowhere to land.

The kids were laughing. She looked to her older brother and sister for help. The twins were laughing, too. Finally, she looked down and saw soft folds of skin exposed to the world. No, it wasn't her skin, she decided, it belonged to someone else. She was not going to let herself be exposed; she let go. This ugly mass of flesh the world could have. Look at it and jeer. She began to laugh with them. It was a funny joke after all! She stepped back and became one of them, mocking the little girl.

When they let her go, Sophia sped down the street toward home. Mrs. Lewis was in the kitchen doing dishes. Tears gushed as she threw herself into her mother's presence, explaining what had happened.

"You asked for it," was her mother's reply, "always trying to get attention. You started it. You should not hang around the twins and their friends anyway. They are not your friends and you don't belong in their group."

On other occasions, the same group of children would chase her as she was going to her girlfriend's house to play. She had to run but often the gang was right behind her. She tried to make it before they could grab her clothes, her head racing with her legs, chest pounding. Fear. Across the lawns the older boys chased, reaching for the elastic band on her shorts. When they succeeded, she fell to the ground, and down went her clothes. The gang huddled around, mocking and pointing. She would black out their images. Back home, she knew Mark and Molly would tell their mother that she started it again, and she would be punished for causing a scene.

Sophia loved feeling nothing and descending into a numb place. Control. She switched it on and switched it off. She could sit high in the chair as the master technician, directing all the movements of feeling, filtering out all the bad ones. Going numb was her protection.

On afternoons when she couldn't face the aggressive group of Mark's and Molly's friends, when her fear was so great that she could feel it, she stayed home and hid. Secluded, their backyard became the courtyard of a castle, with secret entries among the trees, for make-believe family and friends. She wanted to be with neighborhood friends but sometimes it was easier to play alone, pretending. She felt safer.

One evening, at the dinner table Sophia sat alone with her unfinished meal. Her insides were at war. Tears rained onto the plate, floating orange gelatin into the goulash hot dish, macaroni gnarled around pieces of quartered onions and globs from canned whole stewed tomatoes. She knew she had to eat it but her stomach refused the chunky, fibrous stuff. The glass of milk was also going to be a problem, how to get it down without vomiting. Mrs. Lewis said she'd always been obnoxious about eating, from infancy spitting up and screaming through the night.

This night Mrs. Lewis would again relinquish her difficult child to her husband. He would be home soon and get out a board, a cord, or his belt, drag her by the hair or ears from the table, pull off her clothes, and beat bare flesh. While they waited, Mrs. Lewis yelled over to the table from the sink, warning of his imminent arrival. They were alone. Mark and Molly had long been excused to go play in the family room. If only Sophia could get the food into her mouth without any feeling. She felt her resistance, her nausea, her evil welling up within herself.

Mr. Lewis was often absent from dinner. He went visiting after work, and when they were young, on rare occasions, the three children accompanied him on social calls. From the living room of a strange house, Mark and Molly, about six, and Sophia, about four, would sit on the couch, not saying or touching anything, not daring to disrupt the adults chattering in the kitchen. They could hear dishes rattling; the woman was serving Mr. Lewis coffee and dessert or dinner. Their conversation was loud and friendly, and they seemed excited to be together. Later, bypassing the kitchen, the children were ushered out to the backyard to play and again wait. As night approached, they tumbled over each other in the fallen leaves of autumn, playing on an unfamiliar lawn.

Suddenly the three heard a motor; the Lewis family car was leaving. Mark dashed out of the leaves ahead of the girls, through the trees, down the driveway, and out into the city street. He was racing after the car, screaming for his father to wait. The girls followed as close behind as they could manage. Flashes of abandonment pumped adrenalin into Sophia's legs: images of being lost in the strange neighborhood, never finding home again. Mark, a faster runner, grabbed for a door handle as the car backed out into the street, just before acceleration. He struggled desperately to get it open, pulling with all his body strength and clenching his fist. It was locked! The car did not stop but continued down the street. Mark, Molly, and Sophia stood together in the center of the street, watching their dad disappear from sight, terrorized, panting empty breaths, hearts pounding.

After an endless few minutes, the car returned as suddenly as it had gone, the front door on the passenger side was pushed opened. As they climbed into both front and back seats, Mark's composure crumbled into a flood of tears. Sophia sat expressionless, not daring to cry. Mr. Lewis roared with laughter at the cleverness of his joke. It felt worse than the times when he really did forget and leave them.

Usually they were not with him in the evening. By late evening, when he arrived home, they had long since eaten noodles, rice, or pancakes, and gone to bed. Their dad did not eat as they ate on those nights. However, they felt relieved, having avoided his commanding presence and unpredictability.

Parenting alone in the evening, their mom readied her three children for bed. She was often frustrated with Sophia because she, still preschool but toilet-trained, wet the bed. Sometimes her mom's remedy was to diaper her, hoping the humiliation would motivate change. In disgust, she placed Sophia on the floor next to the others, naked and with her legs straddled open, in ridicule and with mockery. Naked and ashamed, Sophia would hear her mom scorn her daughter's lack of control, "You have no respect for anyone, Sophia. Why do you drink so much at dinner and then wet the bed every night? Don't you think I have enough to do? What a smelly habit! Why can't you be like your brother and sister? Disgusting, wetting the bed at your age!"

Mark, looking on, echoed her words, "Sophie is a baby! Sophie still wears diapers! Why do you make so much work for your mother, Baby Brat? Can't you see she's busy enough? What do you care about – no one but yourself anyway!"

Sophia was too old to lie naked, legs spaced. She wanted to cover herself but was told privacy was not guaranteed; it was offered as a prize for when she learned not to wet the bed. In anguish she tried to devise a plan: to never drink liquid again, to stay awake all night. No matter how hard she tried, her plans never worked.

Wet. Cold against her body. Disgusting herself with her own smell. She would awake in the morning no longer a baby, yet not quite a girl.

Pajamas on and readied, they gathered on the sofa together for Bible stories and memory verses.

As they sang, "Jesus wants me to be faithful, to live for him each day; in every way try to please him, at home, at school, at play," she would vow to try to please God, even though it seemed she constantly failed - at home and at play.

When they recited John 3:16, "For God so loved the world, that he gave his only begotten son, that whosoever believes in him should not perish, but have everlasting life," Sophia pondered what would happen if she really did please Jesus and went to heaven with her family. She was afraid of life, of living -- each day. Would eternal life, she pondered, be an eternal humiliation?

When time came for good night kisses, Mrs. Lewis would say she was too ugly, and turn her away. Mark was kissed, Molly was adored, but if Sophia reached for Mrs. Lewis, her mother would make a face, "Ugh," and push her away.

If Mr. Lewis was home, Sophia was kissed – more than the others. He took Sophia aside, smothered her lips with his own, and rolled his tongue in her mouth. Refusal was out of the question.

Since Sophia had made her bed each morning in shame over a wet sheet, she climbed back into the smelly dampness of urine. A sweet-smelling and dry bed seemed an unattainable luxury. Cover-up, accept, pretend, be still, were her goals.

In bed Sophia faced the wall, as directed. When all was hushed, sometimes Mark called her into his room. How she desired to be Mark's friend. Maybe if she could learn to be like him, her mother would love her, too. She knew anything he wanted was O.K. Past the night light in the hall, she could see the lamp on in his room. From downstairs, Mrs. Lewis didn't know they were awake. When Sophia entered, Mark gave commands, with the fierceness of an officer.

"Sophie, stand at attention."

Sophia giggled, saluted her brother, and stood tall, feeling important to him, for a change. Quickly, Mark grabbed her pajama bottoms and underpants, pulling them down to the floor.

This night, Mrs. Lewis hadn't put on the diapers. This night, Mark wanted a look-see anyway.

Everything inside Sophia stopped. She couldn't move. Mark pointed and stared wide-eyed at her nakedness and laughed. She smiled, then laughed, until he was done and released her to return to bed. Trying not to feel anything she pulled up her pajama pants and went to her room.

In bed Sophia still felt violated, naked, exposed, repeatedly dreaming of being undressed. As she grew older and matured, Mark would call her to his room, order her to lie on the bed, then he would lift her pajama top while he massaged. Humiliation. Afraid, she could not refuse. Mrs. Lewis took Mark's word over Sophia's. Mark had power. Molly had privilege to be excluded from his violations.

Sophia hated sleep; she often couldn't sleep. Going to bed meant feeling powerless. She couldn't control her bladder, her dreams, and her privacy. She stared at the wall and stayed awake, eyes peeled, as long as she could. Later, she would make it a practice to become very exhausted before dropping into bed, always tired but never quite able to sleep.

In the stairway one night, Sophia sat in her pajamas in the dark, peering into a ray of light beaming from the main floor. Beyond the darkness, she saw a man and a woman, arguing and fighting. Her insides told her to take care of them, "You are wrecking their lives."

There was screaming, loud screaming, from the woman; then yelling, deep yelling, the man. He twisted the woman's arm and threw her across the room. Thud. She screamed again. The man grabbed her hair and smashed her head against the wall. Another scream. The woman beat the man's arms and his shoulders with her fists, her teeth clenched, words flying.

"You don't care, you won't do anything about our situation. I hate you!"

"What about all the money you spend on junk, you and your high-priced lifestyle! Haven't you ever heard of a budget? Why isn't there any organization in this place? It is either festivity or fast around here! You and your extravagant folly! Fancy meals! Showing off!"

"We don't eat fancy! You call this fancy, rice and potatoes? What about all the money you give to the church? And orderliness? Look who is talking! Why can't you get things done around here after work! Why can't you even show up for dinner after work? When have you organized your time? And maybe if you worked a little harder at your job, we wouldn't have to starve half the time!"

"That's God's money and you know it! Worldly woman! You want to take on God? I dare you! You know what the Bible says, 'Wives, submit yourselves unto your own husbands, as unto the Lord.' If you were supportive and submissive as a wife, I would be able to get more work done!"

The screaming and yelling wouldn't stop.

Sophia's little girl insides said, "No, no. No, no, no."

She was immobilized, but her insides trembled, "Don't bring attention. Don't express yourself. Don't be yourself. Don't be. Fade."

She told her insides, "I want to numb. I want the death I feel. I'm afraid to breath."

When Sophia's dad's hands moved, when there was any movement of his body, he had to be watched. Sophia had to guard, to duck, to numb herself. She could prepare to be numb. Her dad's movements were quick, but she could numb quicker, switching off all the circuits, and turning out all the lights so nobody was home.

It made her father even more angry to have no response. He moved faster and hit harder. If Sophia cried, her dad would say, "I'll give you something to cry about," and hit her more.

She believed that if she did not respond, she won.

Sophia felt her numbness could always outlast her father's energy until night, when he surfaced out of the shadows. She was not numbing. She was not watching, she could not see him, but he came. Her father would penetrate the darkness, the covers, and her pajamas. He would find her. No barrier kept her father out.

Sophia hated sleeping, she hated going to bed, she hated letting go. She decided she must stay awake her whole life. She must stay awake. When they were alone, her dad's body atmosphere was palpable, visceral and mesmeric, powerful, energized electrical - shocking - explosive, terrifying and hurtful. His was a subtle but thorough violence. Her father was afraid but persistent. He spoke of God in evil timbre. He was hidden but exposed. Clean with the scent of aftershave but filthy. Talked much, never saying anything. Loud but silent. His eyes were sparkling and silly as he smiled wryly into her deepest agony. She felt he was an invading army who could not conquer enough. He had needs. He had desires. He had the commandments of God, "Honor your father." Submit.

Sophia remembered being with her father in the shower, the water dripping down, especially on her father. Sophia stood away, she could not see his face. He was looking down at himself, getting ready. She saw what he was doing. She saw his parts, three. They were grandiose, and one was especially large and extended straight while the other two were suspended, floating in their roundness, but hanging down just the same. His parts emerged from a jungle of brownish wiry mass, dripping water beads from the shower, glistening red overtones in the light. He was busy. She was terrified.

Sophia stood away until they approached, the three, and blocked out all her view and covered up her face and filled her up. Standing, she was very young and hardly tall enough to reach but they filled her up just the same. They rubbed on her face blocking breathing, blocking sight, blocking thought; perception became a thread. She wanted to put her thumb in her mouth to keep them out, but her thumb was not allowed in her mouth. No, he filled up her mouth.

The skin was hot; she liked warm skin. She wanted warm feelings. She hated her want, she hated feeling. She wanted to be good, she wanted her dad's love. She hated her desire for goodness, her need of love.

Sometimes her uncle, Mr. Lewis' brother, was there too, and he could do it just like her father; she was preschool age.

Alone, in her little girl dreams at night, red plastic things were provided to relieve her of her job. They were thick red plastic covers that could hold the three parts. Molded, shiny, rubbery, bright red plastic, they were made to go over the parts and collect all the milk, so she wouldn't have to. Just like the red things on milking machines they used to put on cows at the farm, these imagined red plastic things would collect all of her father's milk for her, so she wouldn't have to worry about it anymore. They'd cover her father's parts, her uncle's parts, and they'd do her job for her, the red plastic things. Her father and her uncle could wear them all the time - in the shower, under their pants, no one would know. In her dreams, the men liked the red things because their parts felt warm and good inside, enclosed. Mr. Lewis and his brother were content. They felt cared for. She had done her job.

* * *

So far, all the club members of Bonfire Books were keeping up with the three chapters a week reading. On Friday, they had anticipated the discourse of their group about what actually lies beneath a tightknit religious and seemingly civil society. O'Brien's tale had touched a nerve that all too often could be found in the news of late – maybe not in Sunnyside, but certainly in Chicago and beyond. The Sunnyside folk found it disturbing that the fictional father in the story was finding cover and freedom for his perversions under the pretense of providing leadership and financial support to the church. Furthermore, the mother was loyal to the predator while oblivious to her children; she was focused on her social standing in the community and being in the inner circle of the church people via her scoundrel husband. She felt she had married up and she would uphold that elevated community ranking at all costs. Obviously, the main character was eventually going to be fine, as the story begins with her as a successful adult looking back and thanking God for change.

The Bonfire readers looked forward to the upside of this journey, when the child who made it out would eventually find her way and thrive as an adult. Beyond surviving would be the opportunity for amazing resilience, personal growth, and promise, as evidenced in the stories from the practices of many therapists and social workers. With Charles Dickens in mind, the Bonfire readers had great expectations.

Chapter Seven
Jake & Stella: At Night

Friday, October 5th, 8:30 p.m., Stella texted Jake: Bonfire went long. Leaving soon.

Jake held his glass of wine in the light of the fireplace, then sipped, as he waited while Stella showered and readied for the rest of the evening. Their Friday time was always full of warm feelings and closeness, with no shop talk allowed, only sharing about themselves and the children. Actually, more about each other than the children. No case or law conversations. Tonight, however, what Jake did not know yet was that at some point in their blessed and sacred Friday evening together, his dearest Stella was about to break that rule.

Jake was already showered and clad in a light, loose robe, relaxing on the couch in front of the fireplace. He threw on another log. Their master suite was the one luxury Jake and Stella had indulged in when they purchased their home in Sunnyside. The seating area for two on a couch in front of the fireplace was where they would share a bottle of wine together and decompress at the end of the week. Jake had lit aromatic candles on the marble fireplace mantel and kept the lights dim. Soft music played from his iPod on the side table. He spread out his legs across the carpeted floor and under the coffee table while snuggling down into the comfy sofa.

In their master suite, the ensuite His and Her bathrooms meant the couple were out early in the morning without getting in each other's way, and they could ready for bed separately at the same time. Two closets? Irrelevant, one would do. But the two bathrooms were each designed personally and kept everybody

fresh, punctual, and peaceful. Stella had an oversized tub with
jets as well as a separate shower. Jake had a shower with
multiple showerheads for a massage. He kept his shave
paraphernalia on the counter in his bathroom. Stella left her
make-up out on a tray in hers. In the suite, their bed was queen-
sized, not king-sized – again, largesse was not necessary there.
There were side tables and a lamp for each sleeper. The walk-
in closet was shared and organized. Finally, the couch in front
of the fireplace was usually where the romance began before
they ended up side-by-side, warm sensitive skin-to-skin in bed
later.

"How was the game?" Stella asked as she settled into Jake's
arms on the couch.

"Fun to see everyone. The kids met up with their friends on the
sidelines. Everyone had hotdogs and hot chocolate. Ben kicked
a soccer ball back and forth with Lucas from his soccer team.
Sunnyside lost – no surprise there," Jake replied. "What
happened at Bonfire?"

"Well, Jake, as you know, we are reading an intense novella
about prevailing over childhood distress. In tandem, we are
studying the work of Fredrike Bannink with regard to success
in life over suffering. Apparently, trauma is neither where the
journey begins, nor is it where it ends. Thriving in the worst of
circumstances is an eye-opener - for the rest of us," Stella
shared.

"Who is Bannink?" Jake was curious.

"She's a clinical psychologist from the Netherlands who
promotes the well-being theory (from the research of Martin

Seligman and other founders) as opposed to the forever scarred, needy, and defective standpoint – and then rippling through generations forever, too. To the contrary, her group focuses on solutions, outcomes, and strengths, no matter what circumstances one has come out of. Some call it 'the future with a difference', building positive relationships and personal achievement. Makes sense. We are not what we've been through. We are what we make of ourselves. We can redefine ourselves through quality relationships and successful accomplishment."

"Sounds deep," Jake noted. "But then, with you Stella, it's probably just barely scratching the surface of that immeasurably brainy intelligence up here," and he gently touched her head.

"It's practical, Jake. The only way out of trauma is through it, not sweeping it under the rug. But to do so in recognition of strength, grit, and resilience is the way to go about it. Suffering can be a black hole, where no good outcome seems possible, and supposedly rippling on down through the generations forever and ever, like a room full of mirrors," Stella remarked thoughtfully.

"In which case, it's a money-making growth industry for all of the so-called do-good helper professionals. There's no way out and only never-ending dependency in sight, including down through the generations. Sign me up for that type of job security and money venture," Jake said sarcastically.

"That's the other part of the work by professionals like Bannink. They make their therapy cost-effective because they see less and less of their clients as the clients realize potential and build on their strengths with greater independence. It's positive, upward and onward," Stella added. "Their case evidence reveals growth, character, and self-assurance after traumatic experiences. These experts have confidence in, and high regard for, the people they work with."

"Thanks for sharing, lovely Stella," Jake said softly while stroking her hair. He leaned over, eyes closed, and planted a light kiss on her lips. There was a silent pause.

"Thanks for your interest, Jake. The novella we are reading is a bit tough to talk about – even as fiction. We're looking at a problem that's out there in real life some place. But it's good we are solution-focused, not problem-focused. It's not about sensationalism and gawking over 'poor them' in a story," Stella articulated. She stopped to take a deep breath and then continued, "Speaking of solutions, dear one, there's one more thing I need to share, and this is most important."

Another pause, a sigh, and then, "OK, I'm listening," Jake did not open his eyes.

"There has been some activity going on at the office this week and I need your help," Stella said, switching topics.

"Listening," Jake said.

"As you know, I've had an early morning appointment every day this week with a different member of the Cheer Squad at the high school. You probably saw all five at the football game tonight."

'Probably," Jake followed.

"The girls are very concerned that one of the graduates from last year went off to the University of Illinois in Chicago and now is not answering their calls, since last weekend. They think she is missing," Stella stated.

"After only one week of not answering calls?" Jake asked.

"They've been in touch with her every day since she left for school. Her name is Jade Johnson and she was actually the Cheer Squad leader last year," Stella added, updating Jake on the story.

"Where are her parents in all this?" Jake asked.

"There's some division in her family right now. She is a star student, an excellent athlete, a mentor to the younger girls – and a Christian Bible study leader. This is out of character for her, the home-town girls say. They are very worried," Stella said with sadness.

"What can we do, should we even get involved?" asked Jake.

"The girls, who are her friends and Bible study mates, want us to use our Chicago connections and try to find out what is going on. I was thinking about that guy you know from our Chicago days. He works with law enforcement on cases and he knows detectives. Maybe he could poke around and find out information or at least how these girls can be better informed. Perhaps find out if they can file a Missing Person's Report with the local police," Stella suggested.

Jake opened his eyes and he did not look pleased. He was not thrilled about this. "Get involved in a situation with a college girl that we don't really know?" he asked Stella, looking her in the eyes. "Can there be anything worse?"

"You know that people go missing, and when others don't care, they simply disappear. Families have problems and do not always pay attention, for various reasons. However, the Cheer Squad girls are her Christian sisters and they really care. They are asking for a simple favor. Just go to Chicago on Monday, Jake, and ask questions with your guy there," Stella pushed her point.

"Goodness, Stella, this just seems so out of the blue. I feel like I know nothing about this," Jake admitted.

"I know, Jake, but that's how we feel in our book club. We are learning about what happens to little girls who are growing up and we don't know anything. But Jesus asks us to care, doesn't he?" Stella asked.

"Oh my, Stella. Jesus," Jake whispered.

"It's really all for him, isn't it? The one tossed to the side of the road and we do not just pass on by?" Stella inquired. "When we're walking along doing our own thing, we never know when we'll come across a casualty. God knows, Jake. Don't you think the Cheer Squad girls came to us because maybe God has a place for us in all this?"

"It's really out of my league, Stella," Jake confessed.

"True, but if God has tapped us on the shoulders, he can guide us through this. Right now, all I am asking you to do is to go to Chicago and talk with your friend Richard Van Wagner, so he has his antennae up in Chicago. People go missing and if nobody cares, it's as if they never existed. There's that case in Australia about a teacher that was missing for several decades, and no one seemed to know what happened. More recently, there was the story of the Bear Brook barrels found years ago containing a woman and three girls. No one even knows who they are. This is shameful, unbelievable. The Cheer Squad girls care and want our help. Can't we at least try to help them? Can we care enough to ask questions with the connections we have? That's all that the high school girls are doing – asking questions. That's why they came to see me this past week."

Jake knew Stella had a point. "Monday. I'll see if Richard can see me on Monday. Smoke and Brew, that ribs and craft beer pub in Schaumburg, this side of the big city. I'll hit the road after checking in with Ellie at the office after she opens, then meet Richard for an early lunch, and be home for dinner. I guess we'll just go from here, Stella, with the little we know."

"And ask questions," Stella added. "Just ask questions. Thanks, Jake. Love you."

"Love you, too, Stella. And I'd like to be true to that right now, magnificent woman," he replied.

Jake placed his long arms around the frame of his dear lovely lady, tenderly picked her up, and placed her gracefully in the middle of the bed. He silently put out the candles on the fireplace mantel. Then he slowly, gently put himself beside her in bed. Jake reached back and pulled the string on the side lamp next to his side of the bed to extinguish the light. It was a beautiful night they shared together.

PART II

Chapter Eight
Smoke and Brew

Monday, October 8th, 7:30 a.m., Jake texted Van Wagner: ETA 11 a.m.

At about 7:30 a.m. on Monday, Jake drove his slate gray Silverado across the Gateway Bridge from Clinton, Iowa where he passed over the Mississippi and entered Illinois. He had already kissed Stella and the children good morning and good-by at their house. He had stopped by their business, Legal Grounds, to pick up a coffee for the road and check in with Ellie and the interns. He had texted his Chicago attorney friend, Richard Van Wagner, to once again confirm the meeting. He had checked the drive time and route for road conditions and traffic. However, he had not yet formulated the talking points he would bring up with Van Wagner. Jake had the road trip for ruminating and formulating. It would be about a two- and one-half-hour drive to the Smoke and Brew Pub in Schaumberg, just west of the Chicago metro area, and conveniently reached by highway driving. Jake planned to arrive plenty early. Racing along, he was deep into silence and absorbed in thought.

Behind him, Clinton, Iowa was in full swing with Monday business and preparation. At a distance, there were commuter planes in the air already on the way to landing at the small but busy Clinton Municipal Airport (KCWI), several miles southwest of the central business district. The terminal would officially open at 8 a.m. Tug boats pushed linked barges in both directions up and down on the Mississippi River, passed the two islands that Jake drove over: Little Rock Island and Willow Island.

Even the town of Clinton had road traffic this Monday morning, going in and out of Iowa on the elegant suspension Gateway Bridge. In addition, the railroads, dating back to the Gilded Age in Clinton, were busy with train traffic day and night. Clinton, Iowa had the good fortune to be a river town, a railroad town, and on what was once a major highway, as well as be blessed with a modern little municipal airport that the area's successful industries and residents used for their enterprising connections all over.

Back in the day, Clinton was once rumored to be the city with more millionaires than any other city in the United States. This initial wealth was in large part due to the river, roads and railroads intersecting and then passing through the humble little Midwest town. Logs came floating down the Mississippi that were then shipped out across the nation initially by rail and later by truck over highways. Lumber also provided the raw materials for the lumber mills onsite in Clinton. Finished product could easily be shipped and sent to market out of the unassuming town. In addition, the rich soil west of the river towns supported a large agricultural community that was developed over time. Fast forwarding from the industrial revolution to present day, the astute community leaders in Eastern Iowa had kept abreast of progress in garnering new industries to reinvent the business climate as modernity replaced some enterprises from the past. New opportunities came forward and kept the area thriving.

Iowans not only built successful businesses and farms on the east banks of the Mississippi. They built beautiful homes, state-of-the-art schools, and lovely parks for the pleasures of all four seasons. They stocked the marina with private boats and yachts for weekend excursions. Just south of Clinton, was Beaver Island, with the Mighty River flowing around it.

In the middle of the Nineteenth Century, there had been over one hundred Beaver Island residents, including a couple of farmers. Eventually, the island became largely a wildlife refuge area set aside and maintained for everyone to enjoy. However, there would remain a few local islanders with private summer cabins. Camping, fishing, boating, and sandy beach life could be enjoyed by all in the summer on the Beaver Island paradise. Although it would take only a ten-minute boat ride from Clinton to land on Beaver Island, it felt like another world: the sounds of nature without city noise, sunsets on the river, the smell and lapping of the water, surrounded by flora and fauna and a few friends or neighbors. Because everything had to be hauled in by boat (no different than down through the ages), the material world was left behind for campfires under starry nights.

Jake traveled on Highway 30, the Lincoln Highway, which fully crossed the United States from Lincoln Park in San Francisco to Times Square in New York City. The famed Lincoln Highway was one of the earliest transcontinental highways for automobiles across the United States of America. Conceived in 1912, and dedicated October 31, 1913, it originally crossed thirteen states and ran directly through downtown Chicago. For this trip, Jake would not travel in to the city proper, nor would he continue all the way to Chicago on the Lincoln Highway. For the initial leg of his journey on U.S. 30 Jake bypassed the towns of Fulton to his north and Como to his south, sliced through the southern tip of Rock Falls, and then met the major interchange of Interstate 88, a tollway, en route to Schaumberg. The tollway portion of I88, officially the Ronald Reagan Memorial Tollway, grazed the small but notable town of Dixon, Illinois, which was the boyhood home of former President Reagan.

Back around 1828, Joseph Ogee established a ferry and a cabin on the banks of the Rock River. John Dixon subsequently purchased the ferry in 1830, later becoming the namesake of the town of Dixon right there. Later, the Dixon Bridge AKA Truesdell Bridge incident occurred on Sunday, May 4, 1873, when the Rock River Dixon bridge collapsed while townsfolk were reverently observing a baptism ceremony in the river below. The collapse killed 46 people and injured at least 56 others. A coroner's jury ruled that the Truesdell Bridge design was faulty. Then in 1885, a farmhand struck and killed a Bible salesman while they walked together on a Dixon county road. The murderer disposed of the body in a culvert along the road, which became Bloody Gulch Road. When dairy cattle refused to use the underpass to get to a milking barn, and rain exposed a limb, the sheriff questioned and apprehended the farmhand, who went to prison for life. More recently, in April 2012, the Dixon Municipal Comptroller was indicted by a Federal Grand Jury for embezzling $53 million over several decades, funding her quarter horse-breeding programs. Most recently, a 19-year-old student entered Dixon High School and fired shots during graduation practice. The shooter was pursued and taken into custody by the School Resource Officer of the Dixon Police Department.

From small town to small town, Jake journeyed to his destination, the urban metropolis of Chicago.

Jake pulled into the parking lot of Smoke and Brew in Schaumburg early, as was his habit. He would ask the host to seat him in a back booth with a coffee where he would jot down a few notes before his friend arrived. The pub was not listed as a premier rib spot in the Windy City. Chicago was known for ribs, without question. However, Jake felt quieter and a bit on the west side of the city would make their meeting more user-friendly, and a bit easier for his in-and-out on a Monday. He would be getting back to Sunnyside at a decent hour to wrap up the day and be home in time for dinner.

Although the pub had a full bar, craft beer was the preferred libation with the smoky all beef ribs or brisket or prime barbecue, tender, rich and lathered with tangy sauce. Jake knew the ribs were super meaty, flavorful, falling from the bone, rubbed in a seasoning blend and slow-cooked over a wood-burning fire. The smoky flavors really came through. No reason to settle for a mediocre lunch. Jake would pick up the tab, as he wanted to show appreciation to Richard for the favor for Stella and him on their quest on behalf of the Cheer Squad. They weren't charging the girls, but their benevolence project would have limited imposition on others.

Jake glanced around at the nearly empty pub. He knew that the sports bar had an animated afterwork and weekend crowd of regulars. Scheduling his meet-up for an undisturbed weekday lunch and early afternoon, before happy hour, he hoped for great food, good service, to get something done, and have a good talk, especially since it was Monday.

Richard arrived in short order and took his place across the booth in the back. As soon as they had greeted and ordered from their server, Richard began with questions of his own. "So, Jake, you mentioned that this is about a young lady. I thought you gave up cavorting with the young ladies when you found Stella. Aren't you a little old and passed that now? This isn't the lead-up to a mid-life crisis, is it?"

"Actually, I'm on a quest as a favor to my lovely bride, Stella. She has had five Cheer Squad high school girls from our little town meet with her in our law offices about a friend formerly on their Squad, Jade Johnson. Jade graduated last year and came to the University of Illinois here in Chicago for a business degree. However, it is only October, and it seems Jade is nowhere to be found," Jake explained.

"College girl? New in the big city from her small town? Maybe she found a boyfriend or other things to do. Maybe she has moved on from her small-town friends, and her small-town life," Richard offered.

"Those are easy assumptions, my friend, however, Jade doesn't seem like that type of girl. As a matter of fact, according to the Cheer Squad girls, Jade was their mentor on the straight and narrow. She even put together a weekly Bible Study for the girls, directing their focus to God and purpose," Jake countered.

"Those Bible types can be the ones that fail most miserably once they get in the real world, Jake. You know that as well as I do. Read the headlines about what goes on with some ultra conservatives, and their family values, purity, grand leaders, and mega churches," Richard noted.

"Understood," Jake agreed. "However, my wife, Stella, would like to honor the Squad's request to look into this."

"What about the missing girl's family? Where are her parents in all this? Why aren't they here in Chicago looking for their daughter?" Richard inquired.

"That missing piece of parental concern and involvement is part of the problem. Stella and I plan to visit with Jade's family in Sunnyside this week and find out what is going on. However, time is important, and the girlfriends claim that her parents were unhappy that their daughter chose to go to an urban university instead of staying at home and going to the community college for two years. Family issues," Jake replied.

"The plot thickens," Richard stated.

"It does," Jake concurred.

"So, what do you want me to do for you, Jake?" Richard asked while looking his friend in the eyes with all seriousness.

"Poke around the University and speak with the local police and see what you can find out. Maybe visit her landlord. I have her address here for you, and her cell phone number (which she doesn't answer). I know we are not detectives, and we are doing this as a favor, but Stella insists that this is a worthy cause – it merits our time and effort," Jake insisted. "Often in these cases, it is the squeaky wheel that spurs the police department into inquiry. Someone has to care about this girl. Her friends do."

"I'll see what I can do, Jake, my friend. You can let your lovely bride, Stella, know that I am on her team in this endeavor. You married right, Jake. She is one amazing woman, and you are one lucky guy. Not that you deserve such a beautiful and brilliant partner," Richard added.

"I know, you are right on that one," Jake admitted. "Regarding college campuses, Stella has reminded me of the 2015 documentary called, *The Hunting Ground.* Bad things do happen, undeservedly, to good girls on campus. This is a very bitter truth to swallow when we both have young ladies coming up, Richard. We will face a reality someday, maybe, with the possibility of frightening things happening. Hopefully, safety for girls on campus will improve by the time our daughters get there. It's a wake-up call, you know."

"I know," Richard was of the same mind. "If something happened to one of our daughters, we would certainly want all folks up on deck. Tell your Stella, that I'll start poking around today and be in touch throughout the week. Keep me in on what you find out from the home front, too, Jake."

"Thanks, Richard, and God bless. Greet your marvelous wife, Gillian Lee, for me, and hugs to your adorable little daughters," Jake replied and picked up the check.

Chapter Nine
A High School Star

Tuesday, October 9th, 9 a.m., Stella texted Ellie: SSHS visit. My office ETA: 10 a.m.

Stella was parking her black pearl Honda Accord when she caught a glimpse of a second hour girls' gym class in their navy-blue sweats jogging out of the school and onto the track for a mid-morning run. She remembered her own days at Sunnyside High School in gym class, throwing her head back to breath in the fresh cool autumn air while pacing her loops around the school running track. Athletics were important at Sunnyside, for everyone, even though she was more of an academic herself. With honors, Advanced Placement, and College Preparatory classes, Stella had been well-prepared for her undergraduate degree at Northwestern in Chicago. There was nothing small about high school in an Iowa small town like Sunnyside.

Today was Stella's turn to advance the cause of finding Jade Johnson. The night before, Jake and Stella had briefly discussed what to look for in the high school with regard to Jade and her tenure as a high school student. Naturally, since this was Stella's home town, and the high school was her alma mater, she would do this part of the investigation.

Sunnyside would not be a town without Sunnyside High School. Football, basketball, and baseball were the seasonal games where pretty much the whole town showed up. The high school events took precedent over the NFL, the NBA, and MLB on Friday nights. The marching band performed at the half-time shows and the dance team, dressed in bling and bright colors, entertained. Parents in the booster clubs worked the concession stands like it was a real job, only with friends, and having fun. Stella could not even imagine her childhood town of Sunnyside without Sunnyside High School. As a community involved with the lives of their youth, there was no hierarchy; engagement was egalitarian, all for one and one for all. Everyone pitched in, everyone benefitted. Sunnyside children would have a bright future and it was the job of the adults to inspire, encourage, and demand, upward and onward, of their children to find their place in society and be the person they were uniquely meant to be, that is, socially fit, job prepared, civically responsible, and individually at peace.

Sunnyside High School was where all of the town factions came together as one. There was a diversity of churches – variations of Protestant, a strong Catholic presence, as well as minority groups of Jewish, Muslim, etc., and even some without religion. However, the town came together under one roof at the high school. Yes, there were private schools in the county, but at some point, most families participated in the public-school system. Everyone honored the Common Good of a community with strong academics, a variety of student activities, and respectful civility at the high school. Political parties were kept out of the picture because, again, there was no partisanship when it came to the education of the youth of Sunnyside. Community engagement that promoted responsible citizenship was for all, even if folks approached it from different points of view, and a strong high school was its foundation.

Stella checked in at the front office and took a seat in the reception area, waiting to meet with Beau Christensen. Mr. Christensen had been Jade's guidance counselor throughout her four years at Sunnyside High School. Stella knew him by sight because he lived in the town with his wife, Brielle, and their little firstborn son, Chad. Christensen also coached swimming, boys and girls; most of the staff at the high school coached sports or other activities after school. Some coaches even lived for the coaching while enduring the teaching. Stella had seen Coach Christensen pictured with his teams in the *Sunnyside Times* during the swim teams' seasons. However, this was their first face-to-face meeting. Stella felt he was the person who would have the most information about the all-around student life at Sunnyside, and about Jade Johnson's time in particular.

As she waited, Stella paged through the 2017-2018 yearbook sitting on the low coffee table in front of her. Using the index, she found photos of Jade Johnson that highlighted her involvements during her senior year. Her graduation photo was traditional and lovely. Jade's photo was captioned with, "An enterprising leader where the sky is the limit – so no limits for this senior!" Jade was photographed with the Cheer Squad girls and labeled as the captain. She was a member of the National Honor Society and listed on the Gold Honor Roll for both semesters. Jade had been a frequent volunteer with Service Club projects so there was a photo that captured Jade in a group of students packing food for overseas, even wearing hair nets. In addition, Stella knew from talking with Jade's Cheer Squad friends, that Jade had started a Bible Study for the girls that met on the weekends for Saturday brunch at Sven and Wong's, another restaurant in the Wild Mustang Corral. Leadership, academics, athleticism, service, spirituality, and peer collaboration, Jade seemed to have covered all of the bases as a high school senior. This portrayal appeared to forecast a brilliant future. Why, for goodness' sake, was she now missing?

"Ms. Peltier?" Beau Christensen, asked, stepping into the reception area.

"Stella Peltier, and you can call me Stella, Mr. Christensen," Stella answered. "Thanks for being willing to meet with me on a short notice."

"You're very welcome, Stella, and you can call me Beau," the counselor responded. "You grew up here, didn't you? This was your high school, Stella, correct?"

"Yes, I loved this high school, still do," Stella assured him. "And you are not from Sunnyside, Beau. How are you enjoying our little community?"

"Well, as transplants from Des Moines, my wife and I chose Sunnyside for work and to raise our son (and his future siblings, God willing). We wanted to be in a community where the high school was central, that is, everybody attending the games on Friday, the high school musicals on the weekends, and graduation in the Spring, like this is our past, present and future. As a matter of fact, my wife and I call this place, High School Heaven."

"Your little but growing family landed in the right spot, Beau. My husband, Jake, and I moved back here with the same heartfelt desire. I know people that think that a small town is where kids just cruise Main Street on the weekends and hang out smoking dope and drinking in the parking lot after school on weekdays. But Sunnyside is more than that, I hope you've found. The high school students get their driver's license and their dad's old jalopy so they can do their sports or activities and then get to their part-time jobs. There's quite a variety of positive and interesting activity here for our young people starting out."

"So, you'd like to talk about Jade Johnson, I understand," Beau turned a corner in the conversation. By now they were seated in his office.

"I know she graduated, and she is no longer here, however, the current Cheer Squad members have kept in touch with her at the University of Illinois in Chicago. They are very concerned that they cannot get in touch with her right now and came to our office with their concerns. We used to practice law and live in Chicago, so Jake, my husband, and I are looking into this for them," Stella explained.

"I've heard about this, Stella. Another noted attribute of a small town and close-knit community is that everyone knows everyone's latest concerns and news. What do you think I can do for you right now?" Beau inquired.

"We wanted to know more about Jade to be able to know where to look for her," Stella noted. "You were her counselor, and I know she was a high performing student. What were her aspirations when she was here, Beau?" Stella probed.

"Student information is private, although I'd like to help," Beau said.

"True, however, just in looking over the school yearbook of her senior year, there is a lot of information about Jade that is public knowledge," Stella countered.

"Also, true. Do you have any specific questions for me?" Beau got right to the point.

"I see that she was a leader of the Cheer Squad, a member of NHS, and involved with service projects. I also know, from what her friends said, that she led a Bible Study. Are there any other engagements that you can mention? Jade is focused on business as a major, for example. Was she involved in any businesses?"

"Jade was an intern at HR Wellington's Human Resources, Inc. That was a job and a platform for her to experience a business office first hand. It was an afterschool job, however, both the Sunnyside Chamber of Commerce and Sunnyside High School helped facilitate that opportunity for her. Now that she has moved to Chicago, I assume that ended. However, she gave her senior speech on what she learned there at the Wellington establishment. It was quite compelling," Beau shared.

"Jake and I also have interns at Legal Grounds Café, Beau, however, they are enrolled in the business classes at the community college. I hope they also feel they are having a life-changing experience at our establishment. I don't know, though, it's pretty basic with standard coffee shop chores," Stella remarked. "Getting back to Jade, I wonder how her parents felt about her move to Chicago for her undergrad at the University of Illinois there. I mean, she could have done two years locally, at the community college, and retained her local internship. It would have saved money, too."

"That, Stella, is a question you will have to discuss with Jade's parents, the Johnsons. Jade did mention there were some issues there, however, it is best to go to the Johnson family for insights in that regard. When you connect with Jade, too, hopefully very soon, she can also explain her viewpoint on that decision. Do you know the Johnson family? They have an impressive well-appointed estate somewhat out of town, overlooking the Mississippi River," Beau tried to be helpful while safeguarding student privacy.

"I don't know them personally, Beau, but I guess this will be the chance to do that," Stella returned. "I really appreciate your help today. And, please, feel welcome here in Sunnyside. Stop by Legal Grounds with your family when you have a chance."

Beau checked Stella out of the building as a visitor at the front desk and then walked her down the clean and quiet hallway to the front door entry of the building. It was still a beautiful day, the gym girls were coming back into the school to shower before their next class, and Stella knew that tomorrow she and Jake would visit the Johnson estate on the river.

Chapter Ten
The Family Estate

Wednesday, October 10th, 4 p.m., Stella texted her mom, Sara: Thx for taking the grandkids. Love.

The couple, barreling down the river road highway in their pearl black coupe, was deep in conversation when they saw the sign indicating the Johnson River Estate coming up. Jake, the driver, turned the corner onto the property and all discussion stopped. They were both speechless. Yes, it was a regal palace, a well-appointed property. This was above and beyond. This was a family solidly committed to their family home life. The Johnson Estate rose up from the banks of the Mississippi River in stately splendor.

The driveway was cobblestone with manicured trees accessorizing both sides as it came to a circle that faced the front entrance. In the center of the round-about was a fountain surrounded by more manicured landscaping. As a matter of fact, the entire property, what they could see from the front approach, was meticulously manicured and cared for.

"So, coachman, you can stop to leave me at the front entrance where I shall tiptoe onto the cobblestone, holding the skirts of my gown, and make my fine entrance to attend the royal ball and meet my shining prince," Stella broke the silence and giggled.

"Dreamy thoughts there, Sweet Dear," Jake smiled and replied. "This truly is a magnificent chateau, isn't it?" Just as he parked the car in the circle, the grand front heavy wooden door swung open, and a gentleman stepped out to greet and meet the couple.

"You must be Jake Peltier," the man said, extending his hand for a firm handshake. "I'm Joel Johnson. Come on in, welcome." He turned to greet Stella with, "I'll introduce you to my wife, Cherise, Mrs. Peltier."

"Thank you, Joel, you can call me Stella, and I look forward to meeting your wife, also," Stella responded.

Together the couple followed Joel into a splendid two-story grand entry, and then continued to follow their host as he led them into an equally grand two-story living room with mostly glass facing the east, overlooking the Mississippi River. He motioned the visiting couple to an ivory-colored leather sofa where the couple sat down, comfortably. Immediately, a woman came in with a tea tray and set it on the low black lacquer table in front of the couple.

"This is my lovely wife, Cherise," Joel stated. "She will serve us tea and cakes as we visit and become acquainted. Your café and law offices seem to be busy and doing well, I hear," Joel added, making eye contact with Jake.

"We are grateful to be able to build a small legal enterprise in Sunnyside while we run the coffee shop. My father and mother, Jack and Sara, as owners of the Wild Mustang Corral, have helped us out. Of course, they're pleased we are raising our children, their grandkids, in Sunnyside," Stella explained, "so it is win-win, and we're happy. I'm glad to be back in my hometown after being away for about a decade."

"And what are your enterprises?" Jake asked, looking at both Joel and Cherise. "Whatever it is you two do, it must be wildly successful because you have a lovely estate here."

"Well, Jake, my bride Cherise is a stay-at-home mom, keeping the home front in sync and kids in line," Joel smiled and threw a glance at his wife. "I was fortunate to be brought up with connections to the lumber barons from way back, before my time. With my part of the inheritance, I have established a logistics business that basically is situated in the Quad Cities, just south of here. I commute there, so we can keep our children in the Sunnyside schools, and stay active in our traditional church downtown."

"How blessed for you and your children, Joel and Cherise. You seem like the most dedicated Christian parents on the planet," Jake remarked.

"That's our goal," Joel proclaimed. "By the way, we know you are here about Jade, our eldest daughter. Frankly, we were clearly dumbfounded and disappointed when Jade veered off the trail in high school, and then later even further off the path, with her college venture."

"Really," Stella said quietly, with a puzzled look. "Jade won high honors at the high school. It seems like you all did a fine job raising a wonderful daughter." She glanced back and forth, looking at both Joel and Cherise.

"Actually, Jade first left our church, our traditional setting, in grade ten. That was a big mistake, having been raised in the faith of her ancestors, in particular of her parents. Pure rebellion. Then, to make matters worse, she started leading a

Bible study among the Cheer Squad at school. In our faith, that is overreach for a young woman to step out and be a leader – without the proper headship approval of her pastor and her father. This was clearly a move of misguided thinking," Joel proclaimed.

Cherise looked at her husband, nodded in agreement, and said nothing.

Once again, Jake and Stella were speechless, but this time shocked, and with no awe.

"Finally," Joel declared, "the last straw was when Jade went off to the big city of Chicago on her own, with no blessing from her church and family. This was her abandonment of everything we have done for her. She could have pursued her business degree at a community college closer to home. No, that was not good enough for her. She accepted a scholarship from the University of Illinois, and away she went." Joel and Cherise both shook their heads in disapproval and disappointment.

"She has a scholarship for her business degree?" Stella clarified.

"Yes, quite sizable. In addition, there's a business in Chicago that is paying for Jade's off-campus apartment as she works for them part-time in Chicago. She is working to be an account manager there to manage some of their more lucrative Chicago accounts, is what I've heard," Joel elaborated.

"That's amazing!" Jake exclaimed. "Aren't you proud of your enterprising and hard-working daughter?"

"Not really," Cherise finally spoke up. "Jade is out on a limb and into things where she doesn't belong. She should have stayed closer to home and under the umbrella of the leadership of our church and of our family."

"Well, you have a point, and you clearly care about your daughter," Jake observed. "You know her friends say she is missing, right?"

"She's been 'missing' from us for several years now, Mr. Peltier," Joel said with a stern, formal and distant tone of voice. "There's nothing we can do. She ran off and deserted us. That's the way it stands."

"Aren't you concerned about your daughter, what has happened to her?" Stella pleaded.

"She left us, her choice. In neither our family nor in our church do we tolerate renegade women. Jade's wayward ideas have the potential to spread like wildfire and poison our godly culture, our community of spiritually-minded and sweetness of heart girls. We have another daughter to raise here and we are actually relieved that we get another chance, without the rebellious influence of our off-the-path older daughter," Joel explained, immovable in his stance.

"Wow," Jake murmured. Again, he was without words. This was beyond comprehension. He looked at Stella. She, too, was overwhelmed and feeling helpless.

In the silence, there arose the clatter of dishes as Cherise reached over and collected the tea cups and cake plates, stacking them neatly and carefully on her oversized hostess tray. Stella leaned forward and helped the hostess, and then rose from the sofa and followed her into kitchen. This is where the women of this house belong, was Stella's impression. She asked Cherise about the marble countertops and the cherry wood kitchen cabinet finish. Anything to keep up the connection while Stella and Jake tried to understand, tried to figure this out.

In the living room, Jake spoke in low tones with Joel, father-to-father.

"Joel, do you think we could put aside the gender roles and church practices for just a moment and think simply about the welfare of your daughter as a person; as a person that someday you will want to walk through your magnificent front door, and spend holidays with your family, and confide in you and Cherise as her parents, and bring her future husband and someday their children here? A daughter that you would love to walk down the aisle someday when she has found her one-and-only life partner?" Jake appealed to the other dad.

"Her mother and I would love for that to happen, the future you paint so elegantly with words and word pictures. However, Jake, I don't know what God you worship, but the God I worship has no time for rebellion. Rebellion is as witchcraft and our daughter has gone completely against our values and the holiness of the God we worship," Joel expounded.

Jake could see that this was futile. At least the Cheer Squad was compassionate and concerned. The religion of this home, however, was another story. Apparently, there was an ideal here that was held above Jesus' command to, "First love God, and secondly, love your neighbor as yourself". A daughter was certainly a neighbor, in close proximity to her parents. And yet, these parents had limited their daughter to a gender role that they believed was ordained by God, only to find that their daughter disagreed and operated outside of that designated role.

Jake and Stella were familiar with the theological debates among Christians about gender roles. However, Jake felt this was neither the time nor the place to engage in that debate. A young woman was missing, and they had to find what happened with her.

Stella emerged from the kitchen and Jake stood up.

"We have church night tonight, friends," Joel said to the couple. "Cherise, if you could get the other children ready, we need to pack up the van and be on our way."

Cherise nodded, then shook hands with Jake and Stella, bidding them farewell.

Together the lawyer couple thanked the Johnsons for their gracious hospitality. They promised to keep in touch with the purpose of building more of a relationship between the two families.

"We should get to know each other, outside of these circumstances. I must say that the chocolate fudge cupcakes were marvelously delicious, Cherise," Jake offered.

Cherise blushed, nodded, and ascended the grand central staircase to find the other children.

Joel brought Jake and Stella to the door and approved, "It would be our pleasure to become more acquainted."

* * *

Chapter Eleven
Bonfire and *Out from the Jaws of the Dragon 4: School*

(Bonfire Books opened their second October Friday discussion night with reflections about the main character, Sophia Lewis, starting to go to school.)

Home away from home was school where Sophia Lewis could find friends, learn skills and strive for approval and acceptance. She worked, unintentionally excelling, particularly in math. However, although drawing came easy, coloring within the lines required a tranquility she did not have. Nevertheless, it was her hunger to have choice that drove her to achieve academically. At school she thrived on the letters "A++" marked colorfully across perfectly completed assignments.

Sophia's best friend in first grade was Amy, a girl who lived up the street and was in the same class. One afternoon when they were playing dress-up in her bedroom, they stopped to look at themselves after they put on their formal wear. Under Mrs. Lewis' satin evening gowns, they slipped down their panties, and held up the long flowing skirts, spreading their legs apart. They peeked beneath their skirts, attempting to figure out the geography of the folds of beautiful pink skin. As they sat quietly on the floor, staring, pointing without touching, and comparing anatomical notes, Sophia's mother Bethany Lewis walked in, catching them pointblank. Immediately Mrs. Lewis scolded, "What in the world are the two of you doing? Why Sophia, you are a filthy little girl - and whose idea was this anyway?"

Amy and Sophia sat speechless - they couldn't remember - it had happened spontaneously.

"Wait until your father gets home, filthy girl! You're in big trouble now! And, Amy's mother will hear about this wickedness!

Mrs. Lewis picked up the girls' regular clothes and threw them in their faces. As the girls hastily dressed, Mrs. Lewis continued, "Amy you get home right now - you girls are not going to be playing together for several weeks."

Amy dressed and raced out of Sophia's bedroom, and out of the Lewis house. Mrs. Lewis dragged Sophia by her hair, leading her to bed.

Sophia became very angry also, at herself, and vowed never to look again, and of course, never to touch herself. There was no excuse for being bad and displeasing her mom. How she wanted to please her mom, be a princess of purity like her mom, and be beautiful, be clean, have good clean thoughts, and Christian ways.

When Amy was no longer permitted to come to the house, Sophia thought it was because they had looked at themselves. Mr. Lewis wanted Sophia to bring her little girlfriends to their home to play, and he requested Amy specifically. Mr. Lewis was affectionate with them.

One day at Amy's house, when at last she had invited Sophia over and Sophia was permitted to visit, Sophia found out the truth. Amy's mom declined the invitation for Amy to play at the Lewis house: "No, Sophia, your dad gives too many hugs and kisses. Amy doesn't like it, and neither do I."

Amy looked at Sophia with determination, "I don't like your dad's kisses, Sophia."

At that moment, Sophia felt dirty. She didn't like it either.

In second grade Amy and Sophia were still friends sometimes, but Sophia was not socially in with the other girls. Sophia had tried to take care of herself, but her appearance and clothes were not like the other girls. She did not look well-kept, loved, and cared for.

In the school library Sophia made friends. Among the shelves, between the covers of books, she found another world, her world - friends, girlfriends, lots of them, Anne of Green Gables, Pollyanna, Caddie Woodlawn, and Rebecca of Sunnybrook Farm. She had clothes like theirs and was invited to their homes after school. They lived on the same street, played together, shared wild adventures. She could depend on them, on the goodness and predictability in their lives. She played in the books, fantasies were her outings, and the characters were her girl pals.

Sophia's time away from home diminished when a younger boy was added to the Lewis family. Sophia had been discovered; she could perform at school. Now she was to perform at home, with endless energy, with household tasks, inside and outside, in all sorts of weather. There was laundry, cleaning, meal preparation and dishes, child care, and even consoling Mrs. Lewis in her mood swings and depression. The older twins, Mark and Molly, did whatever and ran free. Sophia was to be the worker bee and take care of things.

On one occasion when Mrs. Lewis was in the hospital, her friend Donna, a woman of the church, stayed with the Lewis children to take over the home duties. However, in reality Donna supervised Sophia doing the chores and forbidding the child to escape her eye. Desperate for solitude, one afternoon while outdoors taking out the trash, Sophia watched for Donna's absence from the windows of the back of their house. Sneaking to a corner of the yard, Sophia slipped up her favorite tree. Its branches gathered round and held her close. Her heart felt relieved. She sang songs softly in the tree castle. When Donna found Sophia, the woman was angry, but Sophia was ready for her; the melodies of the songbirds, the gentle sway of the wind, and the quiet dreams had been refreshing.

In third grade, Sophia whispered to another student, a classmate sitting at the same table in the school cafeteria, "My dad sleeps with me." The classmate brushed her ear, moved the words away, and motioned Sophia aside. Apparently, the classmate's father didn't sleep with his daughter. Sophia didn't understand. She couldn't figure it out.

That year the teacher seated Sophia with the social outcasts, four low-achieving behavior problem boys. This was a riddle of rejection: what did it mean? Perhaps she didn't fit in with the other good students. At the school spring musical, Sophia wore a secondhand dress with a lowered hem. Disappointed, Sophia admired the other girls who were proudly displaying their designer outfits. Her disappointment angered her mom, Mrs. Lewis. Mrs. Lewis asked the other mothers to compliment

Sophia's dress. Mark and Molly, however, both wore new ensembles.

Sophia, writing about her childhood, paused in her frustration with her need of care, the burden of her body, her physical self that she could not care for. She wanted to take responsibility. She could do her school work. She could not supply her body with what she needed, however. Not quite yet.

A storage bin in the hall closet of the Lewis stately home stored gloves and mittens. As Sophia rummaged through, quickly searching for something with which to cover her hands, she was repeatedly disappointed by remnants of knitted pieces - too small, too worn, holes in them, nothing to keep out the cold of the day. Likewise, there was no head covering. She put her fingers in her pockets and raced out of the house. Her cropped hair (her dad's requirement), provided no insulation from the wind on her neck. She wore a winter coat, but that is all she wore in season. There was nothing on her legs and she wore a skirt, so at midwinter they were cracked and dry, red from frostbite, leathery, used to the cold. Moreover, she reasoned, if she didn't think about her legs, she would not feel the cold. Boots, well, there had not been money for boots for her this year. Her mother said she had to understand there was not enough to go around. Moreover, since she was blessed with abilities why should she have needs met? The others might become jealous. She was to be content and dare not request anything. Refusing to complain, she wanted her mom to care for her, without alienating her mom or making her feel guilty. Shamefully Sophia felt her inability to dress properly and protect herself.

Since Sophia's mom had all but stopped buying her clothes, the chill of winter had become terrifying. Although pretending to enjoy nature and winter sports, to appreciate God's seasonal handiwork, in the cold, Sophia felt Creation invade and violate every corner of her being. God had made the world; she felt God neglect her, hate her, torture her, ridicule her.

One day when she was halfway to school, a neighbor lady picked Sophia up in her car. The lady's eyes stared at the girl's legs. Sophia slid deeper into the seat. The cracked skin on her legs was ugly and there was nothing covering the bare flesh.

"Good grief, child," the lady practically shrieked, "Why are you dressed that way?"

"I forgot," was Sophia's weak reply. If only the car would go faster, the girl frantically thought. She would avoid the lady and her car next time. The criticism and embarrassment were not worth the ride. She'd make it on her own, Sophia determined.

Marching into the modern new school in the morning, Sophia breathed in the smell of freshly-cleaned white boards and buffed tiled floors. It didn't feel good, though. The beauty of the building seemed to mock her situation.

Sophia had made friends with the four boys in the outcast row, helping them to do their assignments, to be well-behaved, and to keep neat their row of shiny desks.

Before the bell rang in the morning, Sophia went down the row, checking their hands and faces, sending them to the bathroom for quick clean-up. They made theirs the best. They liked Sophia and they became a team. This angered the teacher even more. Sophia found she couldn't please the teacher. She hated her name when the teacher said it, like ice dripping out of her mouth onto the floor. When the teacher looked at Sophia, the girl felt like a trash heap. Sophia thought her teacher was pretty and she wanted to be like her teacher. New at their school, the teacher was trying to please the principal. Sophia wanted to please the teacher, too.

But Sophia was different. Being different also meant having a brain that wouldn't stop asking questions and getting in trouble for it. Teachers and parents hated questions. Sophia worked hard to make up for it. The demanding brain constantly craved knowing - she couldn't feel, her brain did all the work. The brain, her survival, her curse, and even with the brain, there was much around her she couldn't grasp.

One evening at home after dinner in the family room, Mr. Lewis was flat on his back on the couch, playing with the youngest boy, Timmy, now a toddler. Mr. Lewis' game was to put the toddler between his legs, and then Timmy escaped by crawling away. Over and over the dad played the game with his little son, putting the boy on top of him so Timmy could crawl down and out, racing away. Mr. Lewis spread his legs apart again and again.

They played.

There was movement inside of Mr. Lewis pants. Timmy grabbed what he saw moving, then yanked and played with it.

Mr. Lewis threw back his head and laughed, eyeing Sophia across the room. Sophia turned away, wanting to leave, not daring to move. She couldn't tolerate looking but she didn't know why. She knew this was their Christian dad, and this was Christian family play. They were playing with the central part of his being. Why did it feel odd and dirty to see it?

The dad and son went on to a new game: tickling each other between the legs. Tickling was also a Christian way of families connecting and relating.

Chapter Twelve
Bonfire and *Out from the Jaws of the Dragon 5: Belief*

(Bonfire Books continued their discourse with comments about how the main character persisted away from home while at school.)

Sophia's fourth grade teacher believed in her. It seemed everything she did was magic in her teacher's eyes, the example of hard-work the teacher held up to the other students. Her projects were often displayed. For the first time in her life, Sophia was a star. Ravenously she soaked up her first year of praise.

At the school Achievement Fair one afternoon Sophia strolled through the booths set up in rows in the gymnasium, steering away from projects displaying electricity. As she passed the wires and currents, she noticed that electrical anything petrified her. A chill traveled up her spine: electricity.

One summer morning on vacation in the countryside, Mark and Sophia had stood gazing at horses, planning which ones they would ride later in the afternoon. Molly and little Timmy were out shopping at gift shops with Mrs. Lewis. Mr. Lewis was near his two other children, chatting with the ranch owner. A fence with little white spools at each fence post separated the children from the steer and the horses. The fence had a string of wire that twisted around the spools and then there was another single wire, this one barbed, on the very top.

At a pause in the adult conversation, Mr. Lewis turned to Sophia and shouted a command,

"Sophie, walk on up closer to the fence and grab ahold of that thin wire, the one running around the white spools. You can see it there, can't you, Sophie? I know you and Mark want to ride a pony later, so go on up and grab a good hold of that wire," he beamed a big broad smile as he stated his order. Mark smiled, too, a churlish grin.

In obedience, Sophia stepped forward and grabbed onto the wire, wrapping her little hand around it, grasping it. Electricity pulsated through her body and through her brain. Everything halted for her. She did not know what to do. She was paralyzed for a second and then her whole body was thrown straight away back to the ground, landing flat on her back so quickly it took her breath away.

Mr. Lewis laughed. Mark joined in the laughter, knowing not to touch the wire. Mr. Lewis had repeatedly given orders to follow which caused shock and pain. Mr. Lewis had frequently directed his second daughter to pain and humiliation and laughter. The girl always responded by following directions. Sophia didn't know how to refuse, and disobedience was not allowed.

On the ground that day, when Sophia came to, there were tears, small ones, that trickled out of the corners of her eyes. Seeing everyone laughing, Sophia then smiled and laughed, too. The joke, it had been a funny joke.

Back at the Achievement Fair, in the art section, Sophia found her own winning project, displaying a series of drawings and paintings. Her fingers gently stroked the blue satin ribbon as she put electricity out of her mind.

This particular afternoon, instead of going directly home, Sophia wandered back to the fourth-grade classroom where her teacher was correcting papers. She knew Ms. Jamison wasn't a fashion model or beauty queen, not even as pretty as her mom. However, when Sophia was with her teacher, she thought maybe she could feel what it was like to be in the presence of a woman who loved children: safe, with warm feelings inside when in the same room with her.

Ms. Jamison was always busy, and always keeping her students busy. There was never enough time for all the learning they had to do, it seemed. Learning and building skills were the focus of her classroom. But as the students' minds and bodies buzzed with activities in music and art, math and science, reading and writing, as well as special projects - their little souls rested quietly inside, blanketed under her care, simply free to be as they were. They felt good about themselves in their teacher's presence. They felt loved.

Ms. Jamison's blue eyeshadow matched her blue outfit. Her shiny blond hair was curled loosely and looked soft. Her voice was businesslike yet calm and soothing.

"Sophia, you know that if your dad catches you after school, you'll be in big trouble," Ms. Jamison warned Sophia. But the teacher did not chase her student away. Together they talked. Sophia dawdled. Ms. Jamison was busy on her computer at her desk. Sophia was hungry for her presence.

Mr. Lewis came for Sophia and chatted friendly-like with Ms. Jamison. How did the teacher perceive her student would get in trouble? Sophia wondered. How was this teacher able to figure out Mr. Lewis when no one else could? He was pleasant in person outside his family.

In the car, guilt and fear assailed Sophia. After she had risked staying after school, Mr. Lewis came home early that very day. Then he had come to take her home. The girl felt her dad's mood. Mr. Lewis was subdued but under the quietness of his voice, the words had sharp edges.

"Why did you not go directly home from school as you have been told? Sophia, you know better than this. Your mother needs your help," Mr. Lewis said with a heavy tone.

The housework and the other children were waiting, and dinner was not on. Sophia didn't know how she would be punished. Would it be her father's belt, a visit at night, grounded to the house, additional housework? In response, Sophia felt the teacher's words, her affirmation, and she held on. Mr. Lewis could not take away what Ms. Jamison had put inside her, Sophia felt. That was where her father could not reach and would not touch.

Normally after school Sophia did beeline it home, passing other children, including Mark and Molly, playing in the neighborhood, riding their bikes in the street.

On an ordinary day when arriving at home, Sophia would collapse on the couch with her sketch pads and a stack of books. From the hallway, she would hear her mom complaining, vexed about her daughter's school activities, "You're too involved. You are so demanding on this family the way you must do everything at school."

As usual, Mrs. Lewis would go over Sophia's list of waiting household tasks: cleaning, laundry, preparing casserole for dinner. Sophia knew what would happen if her dad came home and the work was not done. She also knew her mom could get very depressed, and it was important not to upset her.

How Sophia hurt for her mom during the times when Mrs. Lewis would come to her daughter in the afternoon, sobbing about her lost dreams of youth.

"As a young woman, I gave up my dreams and married your dad; I had wanted to be a successful entrepreneur, but my life came to a dead standstill. Now I wouldn't stay married to your father if it weren't for you children. I want to die, Sophia, I want to die. I don't think I can take this anymore. There's not enough money. He's never home and when he is, he blames me. What am I going to do? There's no way out."

Sophia tried to understand but feeling utterly helpless, she did not know how to respond.

"Ole' Sophie, you have no heart. You're as hard as a rock, just like your dad. You're on his side in all this," the mother talked on. "You don't care about me, or anyone else but yourself. "

Sophia worked harder and made it her job to alleviate her mother's burdens, her hurt. Her mother depended on her daughter, her energy, and her desire for goodness. She wanted her mom to love her, she wanted to please her, but Sophia felt she could never do enough to gain her mother's love. It seemed the greater her mother's demands, and the more Sophia did, the more her mother hated this particular daughter. It seemed that there was nowhere to go for love, but Sophia kept trying. When

Sophia couldn't please her mom, she deplored herself for being unlovable.

The work would not take long to do, but Sophia knew the house would not stay clean. Mark and Molly did not have tasks required of them; Timmy was too young. The house would be in disarray again soon and Sophia would have to start over. Setting body to work, Sophia escaped with her mind, dreaming of a simple life where needs were met, and songs were sung, and children were loved.

Chapter Thirteen
Bonfire and *Out from the Jaws of the Dragon 6: Sensation*

(Bonfire Books ended their discourse with taking note of the main character's strategies of escape while going through fire.)

As the number of children had increased at the dinner table, the four children quarreled over who would sit next to their dad, Mr. Lewis. The seating arrangement was paramount, distance from their dad and the quick and sharp thrust of his knuckles being the children's goal. They sat around a solid and imposing oak table that resembled a carved wood piece one would find in a church or cathedral. Mr. Lewis sat high on his throne - he the lion tamer, his children the savage beasts. He portioned piles of starches - potatoes, rice, noodles, bread onto their plates. No choice; they were to consume all.

Their spoons became shovels for a construction project; move the pile from plate to mouth efficiently and without hesitation. Their dad's eye, when he was not shoveling his own pile, carefully scrutinized the children's methods. Their appearance, actions, or words mysteriously provoked him. To avoid his wrath, the children refrained from talking or any type of outward expression. In the repressive group silence, Mr. Lewis' voice presided. "Sounds neat," one of the children would occasionally respond to his monologue. It was important to show interest in their dad's stories. They learn to mutter neutral, non-reactive words to prevent their dad's wrath and to discourage conversation, trying to appease him, but keeping safe distance.

Whether Mr. Lewis was present or not, Mrs. Lewis began to take her plate to her bedroom to eat by herself. Eventually, she stopped preparing meals, purchased take-out food for herself, and continued to eat in seclusion. It became Sophia's job to take the place of Mrs. Lewis in cooking, particularly on Mr. Lewis' behalf. However, the hours of Mr. Lewis at home were erratic and unplanned.

Eventually, for the most part, each of the children learned to simply fend for ourselves. Bags of noodles, rice, or white bread were the definition of food in the Lewis household when Mr. and Mrs. Lewis were not entertaining church folk. Starved for nutrition, the children were force-fed starch. Eating was strictly a punishment. To need was to offend.

After dinner one evening, Sophia stood at the sink. Ouch! Her fingers screamed as she rinsed the dishes in hot water. Nerves were shrieking. No cry, she could not make a sound.

Mr. Lewis, leaning over Sophia, was glued to her body but she could not feel him. She knew this was how a young Christian girl learned to do dishes, to be obedient and useful, to love her dad, to serve God, to earn her birthright, to find her place in the world.

Sophia had cleared the dishes to the sink and proceeded to load the dishwater. The other children had left the kitchen with squabbles. Mrs. Lewis had taken her dinner plate to her room and shut the door. Mr. Lewis and Sophia. Always Sophia was left alone with her dad to interact, to intertwine, to mesh. Sophia, his extension, his toy, his limb, at his command.

"You know, Sophie," his voice waned, "the Dawson's oldest daughter comes directly home from school to the kitchen."

It was to be Sophia's calling. Mr. Lewis checked the water running in the sink. Not hot enough. Extinguishing cold, he ran only steaming hot water into the sink. With an iron grip on Sophia's arms midway between the elbows and wrists, Mr. Lewis held his daughter's hands fully submerged in the scalding water and pressuring her arms, so her hands were flat on the bottom of the sink. He boiled the girl's hands.

The girl pauses in her writing, with pain, and the woman joins her, uncovering her own pain.

It was strange how she could not feel it then. She didn't say anything, pinned at the sink edge, hands pressed into the water. Hands red, then white, scalded. Hands cracked, dry, rough. Frostbitten in the winter. Hideous hands she never regarded as her own. He could have them, Sophia thought, they no longer belong to me.

Sophia would eventually feel it one day, the scorching hot, the nerve ends screeching, howling. The inner throb resounding pain. Oh God, she would feel it. Why not then, but later when Mr. Lewis was not there, she was able to feel a dread of hot water, warm water, any dishwater. She used lotion to cover up the past, which was not enough to erase the hurt, the scalding hot water ever running in the sink. They were not hers, those hands, they were not hers.

At age ten, Sophia felt her hands looked like she was eighty years old, leathery, bright red, rough, wrinkled. Her hands stung, except she had stopped feeling them. They were ugly except she had stopped looking at them.

No one else knew how Sophia felt when she touched hot or cold and her entire being had tremors. Was it really the hot or cold or was it only a memory? she would ask herself until she figured it out. She learned to differentiate nerve damage, hot/cold, and memory. She went through the pain of her memory, acknowledged what had happened, and emerged free eventually.

As a child, Sophia had withdrawn feeling to endure whatever was happening, painlessly. However, this wore her down. When she in due course allowed herself to touch and feel, initially the sensitivity was intense and resulted in exaggerated reactions to any sensation. Inner pain seemed to flow endlessly, but in truth it was not endless. It did end. From numbness to excruciating pain to freedom. One day what had happened was brought into the light, connections were made, and Sophia walked away from what had been done to her in the past.

However, as a child growing up in Sophia's world, her sensations were in shock. For her survival, mind and body separated. She would not feel what was overwhelming.

As a child, she couldn't taste. If so, it would have been strange foods in enormous amounts, her dad's saliva, his body fluids.

She couldn't feel. If so, it would have been cold wind and snow, hot sticky skin in bed, fists pounding, lashing boards and cords, electrical currents, scalding hot water, penetrating fingers, tongues, lips, and other parts she didn't understand.

She couldn't see. If so, it would have been the quick hand, the belt, raging faces, smirking stares, scorn at school, disapproval, her nakedness before many eyes invading and plundering her privacy, the emptiness of her own silhouette in the mirror.

She couldn't hear. If so, it would have been screaming, ridicule and taunts, God this and God that to everything.

She couldn't smell. If so, it would have been her dad's mouth, their mouths, a wet bed, soggy sheets and blankets, her dad's body smells, her own body smells – the body she couldn't own and didn't know how to care for.

Eating to anxiety, sleeping to fear, awakening to anger, moving in pain.

The Shepherd holds the girl and the girl loves the Shepherd. He, a man of sorrows, acquainted with suffering, as one whom men did not esteem, understands Sophia. The Shepherd and the girl commune. She continues to share with him her story. She wants to share all. He listens attentively and without disdain.

* * *

At the close of the discussion of week two of Bonfire Books reading of *Out from the Jaws of the Dragon*, Jerry and Louisa Moore, the club founders, guided the group in a reading of Psalm 23, acknowledging the good Shepherd that the novella described. The club then also read together Psalm 10, citing in particular verse 14 in how God cares for victims, and from James 1:27 about faithful Christians' responsibility to orphans. Then they prayed, not just for orphans and victims, but also that those blessed would be faithful to their calling as Christians.

Chapter Fourteen
Jake & Stella: Interrupted

Friday, October 12th, 8:30 p.m., Stella texted her mom, Sara: Checked in, Eagle Point Spa.

Jake was chilling in the hot tub when he heard a key card at the door of their suite. This was expected. It was exactly what he was anticipating, that is, a lovely lady to join him in their room's ensuite spa with a glass of wine. This lawyer at the end of his week was looking forward to a Friday with his sweetheart, relaxing and bringing their romance up to date. The week had been full of events of the business variety as well as time together as a family with the children. Now he would have Stella to himself. A husband might wonder if this was a selfish thought. How Jake loved their times together as a couple with neither law, nor coffee, nor community, nor children. Nor guilt.

"God bless the children, giving Dad and Mom a night off each week, just for themselves," Jake whispered a prayer.

Friday nights kept things fresh and enjoyable between the husband and wife team, even when they had to iron out concerns between them before the sweetness could begin. It happened periodically. From time to time there were things to work through, working through which the couple preferred – even on Friday nights - over sandbagging or building up unresolved conflicts over time. Realistically, working through differences was a part of having two thinking individuals partnered together, building a life as a couple, and a unit as a family. Jake smiled to himself, with a look of deep satisfaction.

This Friday night, while Stella was at Bonfire Books, Jake had brought the children to Eagle Point Park after school for park play and a nature hike. The weather was crisp, in the forties and the sky a bit cloudy. In their light hiking attire, before the snow and higher temperatures of winter set in, the three enjoyed walking a park path, then playing on one of the park playgrounds. Later, the children climbed the stone tower situated high on the bluff in the park. Sticking their heads out of the cut-out openings in the tower walls, the children called to their dad as they climbed the inner spiral staircase. They were also able to look down on the river bluffs at a wide section of the Mississippi from the top of the tower. When they spotted a bald eagle, Jake took out his phone and took photos. After the children descended the tower stairs, Jake reminded them that they'd all be back in the winter snow to cross-country ski the trails in the park on Sunday afternoons – Mom included.

After the outdoor excursion, Jake asked the children for their dinner preferences. The two young ones agreed on the Dockside Café, overlooking the Mississippi, as their first choice. They wanted to observe river traffic while they visited with Dad. Jake was in with their decision, and they did find a table for the three of them, at the windows and facing the river.

Over chicken tenders, salads, and potatoes, Jake quizzed his son, Ben, and daughter, Emma, about school, activities, and plans for the following week. They chatted with enthusiasm at having Dad's full attention and a superb view of the outdoors. Another eagle swooped over the bluff in plain view, and they were all delighted. When his son reached for the dessert menu, upon finishing his meal, Jake took it from his hands.

"Grandma Sara will have lots of treats and snacks at her house tonight, Son," Jake said with a smile. "You want to save room for Grandma's treats, don't you?" His son nodded.

Leaving the Dockside, Jake brought the children to the grandparents' home for the night. They had each pre-packed a backpack for the overnight sleepover with Grandma Sara and Grandpa Jack. Sara met them at the door and scooted Jake off to his Friday night with his bride. Now, the grandparents would have the little ones to themselves for some fun. Grandpa Jack hadn't arrived home from Cowboy Jack's restaurant yet, so Grandma Sara got her grandchildren settled into their rooms, and then brought them into the family room for Games with Granny night.

After checking in at their Friday night reservation, Jake ran the hot tub and jumped in. He had turned on the gas fireplace and put the lights down low. Music played on his iPod. Nothing to do but wait for Stella and think dreamy thoughts.

Jake immediately noticed that Stella had a serious look on her pretty face as she entered their suite and put down her things.

"Everything go well at the desk?" Jake inquired.

"Perfect," Stella answered with a smile. "And I can't wait to get in that hot tub with you, my dear," she added.

Jake waited for Stella to share her thoughts. Soon she, too, was relaxing with him in the swirling warm bubbly waters.

"You know, Jake, my thoughts are always heavy after Bonfire Books on Fridays because we are reading a novella that opens up discussion about the vulnerability of those in our charge in our society," Stella opened up. "It just takes a bit for me to wind down and put that aside. It's critical stuff."

"True," Jake agreed, "And I am proud that you and your club are willing to consider what happens to the weaker ones in our world, and how to be more responsible as fellow citizens."

"Thanks for your empathy, Jake," Stella said. "I'm very fortunate to have you on this journey with me."

Jake put his arm around Stella's neck, and floated his body forward, gently planting a delicate kiss on her lips. They lingered, tenderly, softly, quietly, eyes closed, taking in the moment, hoping it would last forever.

Jake's cell phone cut in on the moment. They ignored it. It kept ringing and went to voicemail.

"Jake, this is Richard Van Wagner with some news for you. Sorry to interrupt..."

As soon as Jake recognized Richard's voice, he leaped out of the tub and grabbed his phone. Soaking wet, his propped himself on the side of the bed anyway, as he answered, putting his device on speaker phone so Stella could also participate. Stella followed Jake's lead, grabbing a couple of towels that she draped around each of them, sitting on the side of the bed. They dripped into the towels. Stella listened in anticipation while Jake intercepted the call.

"Richard, this is Jake," he cut-off the caller.

"Are you sitting down, Jake?" Richard asked.

"I am," Jake answered, "and Stella is here with me. We have you on speaker phone."

"They have found and identified Jade Johnson's body," Richard informed the couple. "So now we have the young lady, but she is dead, and this is a homicide, obviously."

"No," the Peltier couple gasped together.

"Yes," Richard said. "She was folded up in a garbage bag, weighted, and stuffed into a large zipped cloth wheeled luggage bag, obviously thrown into Lake Michigan. But, with her body decomposing, gasses emitted from her corpse brought her to the surface, and she washed up on shore, near the marina that sits between Chicago, Illinois and Gary, Indiana. Naked in there. After a missing person's report was put in earlier in the week, and with the appearance of her body thereafter, they have identified that indeed, this body is Jade Johnson."

"Unreal," Jake said. "We are thankful you are following this with us, however, grieved that this now is a homicide."

"Without a doubt," Richard commented. "The marina has security cameras, her apartment has security footage, and they have searched her apartment as a crime scene. They have her computer, phone, and forensic evidence from her apartment, hopefully. I don't know. They don't say much in an ongoing investigation. No idea what they are seeing, as of yet. We just know that something bad happened, presumably here in Chicago with your small-town girl. The Media covered the appearance of the body – found by a passer-by, the identification of the victim, and the location of her apartment. That's how we know what we know so far. What they found in the apartment, not a clue."

"She was a superstar, Richard, and this is very sad," Stella noted. "From everyone we have talked to, she was as wholesome as an ice cream social, focused, and had high goals. This should not have happened to this girl. Somehow, we are going to have to speak with her friends on the Cheer Squad, if they haven't already heard."

"This shouldn't happen to anyone," Richard added. "They will have to figure out motive, the means, and the opportunity," Richard said. "And then we will have our perpetrator."

"She didn't have any enemies here," Stella said, thoughtfully. "She is held in very high regard in this town."

"Well, something happened here in Chicago," Richard noted. "And it only took a few weeks of living here before she was gone. Hardly enough time to get to know anyone."

"The vicinity of her apartment, is it in a good neighborhood?" Stella asked.

"It's in a very good neighborhood," Richard answered. "She seemed to be in a sensible situation. They are collecting data and forensics right now, tracing her steps and her contacts. Not sure how long her body was out there, as they are not saying much. It's a mystery."

"Well, we will not let this get cold, Richard. We care about each other. Please stay with us on this case, and we'll keep doing our investigation here," Jake pleaded.

"I imagine the detectives will eventually show up in Sunnyside asking questions. They, too, will want to know more about this young college student and her relationships and connections," Richard was thinking out loud.

"I don't know what they think they'll find here, except that she was an outstanding young woman," Stella guaranteed Richard. "They need to take a serious look at their city and what happens to innocent small-town young women who show up to get a good education and have a brilliant future."

"I'm sure they are doing just that, Stella, but I will keep on it and keep you all posted," Richard promised them. "What happens to stellar young women who set out to accomplish great things, and then end up thrown about as trash in a garbage bag – unspeakable."

"Exactly," Jake was adamant. "This is us. This concerns us, and we will see this through."

PART III

Chapter Fifteen
Sven and Wong

Monday, October 15th, 8:30 a.m., Jake texted Stella: Chamber of Commerce, you're up next.

HR Wellington, President, Sunnyside Chamber of Commerce, was at the podium when he made the announcement, "Continuing with New Business, this month we are starting our own Sunnyside Podcast, as 2018 is the Year of the Podcast. We have at the helm, Eleanor Pearson, our lovely intern from the community college, specializing in media and journalism. She will tell you more."

A tall regal college student in a sharp business suit and heels - mixed race, and the best of both - stepped up to the dais as Wellington stood aside. The audience was immediately intrigued and impressed. The electricity of anticipation filled the Emperor Banquet Hall at Sven and Wong's Family Restaurant.

"Sunnyside is moving into the future now and progressing to be going over the airwaves. This is a step in the right direction for this hidden gem of a wholesome little town of great promise and even greater opportunities," the intern began, and then continued with, "Good morning, my name is Eleanor Pearson and I am here to promote your community, and more specifically, your business. My media team will be coming around to your establishments for human interest pieces. We want to know about you, your staff, your business services, and what is your part in the greater community of Sunnyside," Eleanor further explained.

There was polite but enthusiastic applause from the audience. Eleanor paused to take this in. She was pleased with the reception of the members regarding this new venture.

"The Sunnyside Podcast is the warm-up with our Sunnyside Chamber of Commerce New Media Productions. Eventually, we are also going to be filming and posting on a regular basis, videos with visual tours and highlights of our beautiful venue here on the west bank of the Mississippi in the amazing state of Iowa. From audio to visual, we'll cover it all.

Eleanor beamed with pride as she detailed, "We have a strong educational system, preschool through community college. We enjoy recreational and civic activities in all four seasons. We offer a variety of career paths for every type of interest and we're open to innovation. We support a vibrant business community that offers products and services that we want to publicize to the world."

She paused, smiled, and continued with enthusiasm, "Sunnyside community engagement sets the standard as a model for others. For example, I hear there is a dentist that had the property surrounding his dental office building professionally landscaped to be a thing of beauty. Then, he established an award-winning rose garden and a peace garden there with walking paths and garden sculptures. This is ingenious. The dentist and his Garden of Peace will be one of our first human interest stories. He went way above and beyond to add to the tranquil quality of his neighborhood. One of these days, we'll be checking out the peace garden that renders a certain excellence of character to the dentist office building area. Only in Sunnyside."

"But there's more. I heard a rumor going around that come spring, Sunnyside will have a group of engineers and English professors seeking Frankenstein in Europe. Owen and Willow, of Out with Owen & Willow: O WOW! Travel – would you like to stand and speak to this?"

"Ah, ha! Ms. Pearson, you have discovered our undercover operation!" Owen said, eyes twinkling with mystery, as he and his wife, Willow, stood up from their seats in the audience.

Willow described to the audience, her vision circling the crowd, "Next year, we will be on a journey in Europe – the Frankenstein Tour. We will be exploring the mysterious yet scientific connections of Mary Shelley, Frankenstein and Earl Bakken, on a European cruise. If you like science and innovation, as in electrical engineering, and literature and history, as in sci-fi, then this clandestine cruise is for you, my friends. Check out our O WOW! Travel website and pack your bag for an adventure." The couple grinned, again made eye contact all around, and then withdrew to their seats.

"There you have it, Chamber members. Another amazing part of this community: O WOW! Travel. At this point, our media team from the college is ready to hit the town as New Media journalists. We hope you are as excited as we are about this fresh undertaking. See you soon at your place of business." Eleanor concluded her introduction then stepped down and rejoined the audience.

Wellington appeared again at the podium and reiterated his support of the media project, "Ms. Pearson will be contacting you about events and highlights of your part of the mosaic of our greater community. She is ready for any and all taping and filming ideas from you, although she and her team have a few ideas of their own. Be ready for a phone call or an email when she can set up a time to tape your segment. Anticipate more customers and to grow your business. We may be small, but we can impact our world for the better and help you expand your enterprise."

Wellington gazed across the audience, and then moved on in the agenda, "We have one more item – Stella Peltier from Legal Grounds has her turn for a short presentation of her establishment here at the platform. I know she was bringing the children to school, Jake. Is she here yet? I thought I saw her walk in at the back," the President craned his neck a bit to search the room.

Just then, Stella walked up to the front, and Wellington sat down in the first row.

"Good morning, friends, neighbors, associates. As the female gender side of the Peltier Legal Partnership, offices located at Legal Grounds in the Wild Mustang Corral on the east side of town, I'd like to take a moment to address the men in this crowd. The reason, men, you want a lady lawyer is because you know a woman works harder and will see your concerns through with the utmost privacy and dedication."

At this point-blank, somewhat tongue-in-cheek, quick introduction, the row of bankers and financiers seated in the back, all men in suits, chuckled. There were muffled comments and asides among them.

Stella elaborated, "Concerning your property purchases, your business ventures, your prenups, perhaps a divorce, and your elderly parents' estates and wills, yes, I can do business for you while you enjoy your complimentary cup of Joe in the corner by the fireplace, with the ESPN screen over the mantel and the Wall Street Journal on the coffee table, at Legal Grounds. I'm passing out my business card here so you can confidentially get in touch," Stella stepped forward and handed a stack of cards to the first person in the front row of each side of the audience.

Stella then stepped back up to the dais and concluded her one-minute pitch with, "I can get the job accomplished for you, gentlemen, and you know it. So, stop by and get it done."

After delivering her spiel to the Chamber, her turn this week, Stella sat down in the chair Jake had saved for her next to him. She glanced at Jake and he smiled back at his lovely wife while whispering, "Clever, honey. Interesting angle."

In the background, Jake and Stella heard HR Wellington announce, "Concluding our regular meeting of the Sunnyside Chamber of Commerce, I'd like to remind new members that we meet again next week on Monday, the 22nd of October, here at Sven and Wong's Emperor Banquet Hall. Breakfast will be served at 7 a.m. as usual so please remember to reserve online your order as a courtesy to the restaurant. The meeting will begin at 7:30 a.m., featuring our special speaker Brandon Hall, of Green Valley Enterprises. He will be presenting ideas for maintaining our pristine environment here in Eastern Iowa, for a better future.

As the meeting broke up, Jake rose and quickly made his way to the platform to catch HR Wellington before he left for his office.

"HR, may I have a word with you?" Jake asked the Chamber President.

"What's on your mind, Jake?" HR responded.

"It's about Jade Johnson, who interned for your business when she was in high school," Jake answered.

"She did," HR said, as he busied himself with gathering his papers and computer from the podium.

"Well, she is missing, in Chicago," Jake said. "Do you know anything about this?"

"Nothing, but you know, Jake, young girls who go to college in a big town discover that there are all sorts of distractions," HR offered, quickly.

"Jade Johnson doesn't seem like a girl with distractions, does she?" Jake asked.

"We've had many interns over the years, Jake," HR clarified. "Students go to college, and all kinds of things are out there that get in the way of their good plans. It's a fact of life. Things don't always turn out the way we would like for our young people."

"But this is serious," Jake said somberly.

"Life is serious, Jake," HR answered right back. "And so is the fact that young people and life, no matter what sort of opportunities we provide for them, do not always turn out for the better. Now, I have appointments back at the office, Jake. Sorry I can't help you."

HR grabbed his computer case, turned, walked away, and left. Jake stood there, quietly. Stella came over.

"Jake, I thought we could sit and visit with Dave Swenson and Lily Wong for a few minutes before we go back to the office. Although they are closed on Mondays after the Chamber meeting, Dave himself prepared a meal for me since I missed the early Chamber breakfast. They're waiting in their employee break room next to their offices at the back by the kitchen," Stella broke the silence.

"Sure, Stella, love to visit with them," Jake followed her back to the employee room.

Once all four were seated, Lily began the conversation.

"You know, friends, Jade Johnson and our youngest daughter, Julie, were pals in high school. We were sort of the Mom and Pop of the Cheer Squad Bible Study that Jade started. They often met for breakfast here at our restaurant on Saturday mornings. We were so happy that Julie had a fine Christian girlfriend in Jade Johnson," Lily said.

"What kind of girl was Jade?" Stella asked.

"My question, too," Jake added. "HR Wellington – she interned for him, and I just spoke with him about Jade – well, he seems to think that she just disappeared out of the blue because, unfortunately, that's what normal college girls do. I didn't even get into the fact that we now know for sure that she was murdered."

"Let us tell you about Jade, then," Lily said. "Jade was not a mean girl as some high school girls are. She was not materialistic although her parents are very wealthy. She was not seductive even though she was very pretty."

Lily continued, "Jade brought an aura of integrity to the team. She led the group in athletics, academics and also in spirit. She had a deep spiritual commitment to Someone Higher, to her God. In this capacity, Jade turned around the team. Whereas most squads are about flaunting their bodies, showing off their clothes, and putting other girls down, Jade was tender and sweet on the outside while tough and determined on the inside. She felt the squad was the chance to take the girls at school in a different direction."

Lily gave more background to the story, "Not everyone was buying it, at first. Jade was put down before she was lifted up as a role model. She walked through fire in the beginning to maintain her spot on the squad. The others ostracized her, criticized her, and generally made life difficult for her. She was purposely kept out of the social life of the team, not invited to parties, and not included in girl chat. Jade put on her game face and let everyone know she was in it for the long haul. She was not going to be easy to get rid of. In the end, they did not get rid of her, she held her own, and even better, she lifted everyone to a higher standard. It didn't mean that there weren't other girls sleeping with the football players, but it did mean that this was not the high standard of the team. The high standard of the team was to save yourself, be friends (without benefits) with your boyfriend, and reach for a college and career path beyond small town sex and early pregnancy. Jade made it feel good to make better decisions. It didn't mean that she was perfect – far from it. She was privately open with the squad that she had failed herself, but it only made her more determined to carve out a straight and narrow path and walk the line right into college, career, prince charming, and a family life that would make her God, and her own heart, proud."

Lily concluded with, "That is why the Cheer Squad girls showed up, one by one, to let you know, Stella, that something was wrong. Jade seemed to have it all figured out. She had a future. But then she was gone. Last week, no one knew where she was, after having left for the big city and established herself there. She simply disappeared."

Stella whispered, "And now we do know, one thing anyway, she is never coming back."

Chapter Sixteen
Traditional

Tuesday, October 16th, 1:30 p.m., Jake texted Stella: At Riverside Bible Chapel.

Jake was in the church lobby when the pastor walked in. Standing by the church entryway stained glass windows and reading the latest church newsletter. Contemplating questions he would respectfully ask the clergyman. It was Tuesday afternoon when the pastor said he had a little time to see him. As the pastor approached Jake to shake his hand, Jake noted the conventional clergyman outfit Pastor Norstad wore – clerical collar, black clergyman shirt, dark suit, and a very well-appointed watch on his wrist. He could picture the pastor one step further – in a black robe, high in the pulpit on Sunday morning, with his booming and convicting voice resounding throughout the Chapel. Traditional. Curiosity passed through Jake, muted but meaningful, like wind high in the clouds on an overcast day. Attentive, he made eye contact with the clergyman as they connected. Like everybody in the town, Jake had a respectful disposition regarding men of the cloth. However, he had been dreading this moment. He would have to ask the man some difficult questions.

The traditional church struck Jake as a shrine of beauty. There were stained glass windows, depicting scenes of the Christ, throughout the entire building. Particularly in the worship sanctuary, Jake had noticed, the multi-colored stained-glass scenes ran floor to ceiling, with very high ceilings. There was wood everywhere, too. The floors were polished oak, as were all trim and accoutrements. The pews were also polished solid wood, of a different variety. Bright crimson carpet runners covered each aisle to soften the sound of footsteps and protect the wood floors from stiletto heels. The church had been designed with traditional architecture and attention to acoustics for classical music. There was an enormous pipe organ at the front of the sanctuary. There was also a grand piano on the stage or platform, off to the side. A choir loft was positioned in front, off to the other side of the platform. Jake got the picture. Hymns from the Middle Ages were sung on Sunday mornings with solemn demeanor, slow timbre and a four-part harmony ageless choir. There was to be no rock and roll, no primitive dance hall music, in this place. God would have none of it.

The pastor motioned Jake to follow him down a hall, past a receptionist, and into his office. Together they introduced while Jake took in the view in the pastor's study. There were shelves of King James Version Bibles and theology books. On the walls were displays comprised of the pastor's credentials, photos of his hunting trips and guy groups, paintings of Jesus, and more photos – of his family. Pastor Norstad had a lovely wife and his four children looked – perfect. This was a pastor who took God, manhood, the King James Bible, and his family seriously. Jake smiled, but was it in admiration? Approval?

Pastor Norstad immediately opened the meeting with prayer. "'Dear Father in Heaven let us meet here in Your Name and for Your Glory, only. Amen.' Now, what can I do for you, Mr. Peltier?"

"Pastor Norstad, you can call me Jake. Last week, my wife and I visited with the Joel and Cherise Johnson family," Jake got down to business.

"Joel and Cherise Johnson are two of our most prominent members here at Riverside Bible Chapel," the pastor noted. "Their family, and extended families are very involved and committed, over decades and generations. The Johnsons are deeply loyal to our time-honored traditions. They show up to volunteer, and give generously, including to our mission projects. They are the ideal family here at Riverside Bible Chapel. There always seems to be at least one of the Johnson family men on our board. Such faithful gentlemen."

"Then you know their oldest daughter, Jade, is that correct, Pastor?" Jake asked. "There has been some concern about Jade recently."

"Jake, I baptized Jade Johnson after confirmation. I watched her grow up here in our children's programs and she entered the youth programs with great enthusiasm," the pastor recalled. "However, somewhere in her youth, she went astray. She went off on her own and started a Bible Study without the permission of her father, and without the approval of the church. This is not Biblical. A woman – and certainly a young woman - is not authorized to teach a Bible Study without being under the authority of her husband or father, and under the church leadership. Officially."

"The not being Biblical part is debatable, Pastor. There are groups such as The Junia Project that can argue that point much better than myself. However, I am here with regard to Jade Johnson. She went missing after she was at a university in Chicago for about a month. This doesn't seem like her. She doesn't seem to be a risky behavior type of person. I was wondering if you would have any insight about this, Pastor."

"That was Jade Johnson's second big mistake," Pastor Norstad proclaimed, eyebrows frowning. "Her parents wanted her to live at home in Sunnyside to go to community college right here in this area. She ran off to the Big City. Going out from under the authority of your church and your pastor is the riskiest behavior of all!"

"Again, I'm not sure I agree with you on that one, Pastor Norstad. There are cases right now in the church at large, and some specifically being litigated regarding your very own church denomination, where the church was not the safest place, particularly for a young girl in a youth group. Sometimes, it is the youth leader, or another pastor, that has been the predator of a young victim. More and more stories are coming forward. Did Jade leave your church because she was targeted or uncomfortable here?" Jake asked pointedly.

"That is the most ridiculous thing I've ever heard, Mr. Peltier. How dare you come here with such ideas! We have families that have been here for many years, we are a close-knit group like a family, and we take care of our own," the pastor arose in a huff, leading Jake to the door.

"That is exactly what scares me," Jake said, and followed Pastor Norstad out of the office, then proceeded out the front entry, and went to his car.

Chapter Seventeen
Renaissance

Wednesday, October 17th, 9:30 a.m., Stella texted Jake: At Renaissance Campus.

Stella could hear the band playing as she drove into the parking lot. Apparently, there was worship band practice going on in there on a Wednesday morning. She wondered out loud, "How many are hired and paid professional musicians? They're having practice on a weekday morning, during what would be a normal workday for most people. That takes bucks."

The outside of the church didn't look like money, nor did it look like a church. It looked like a Walmart, like a big box store, actually. Yet when she stepped through the double glass doors entry at the front, Stella was amazed at what she saw. There was a classy lounge area with sofas, comfy overstuffed chairs and coffee tables, set against the backdrop of a rock wall that flowed with a soothing, soft waterfall. The surrounding tropical plants in pots and stone plant boxes gave the look of an indoor arboretum.

Stella walked through the lounge area, following the signs to reach the receptionist's office. On the way she passed a coffee shop with several people visiting at tables and others working on their computers at the bar, while sipping on their lattés. A barista was wiping down the shop's counter, ready to take orders.

"Maybe the band will need a coffee break," she said to herself, and kept walking. Screens hung from the ceilings throughout the open areas, flipping through church news, church videos, and flashes of band music videos. In addition, in both the lounge and the coffee shop, there was one wall dedicated to an enormous screen for more than announcements, apparently.

At the receptionist office, Stella checked in, stating that she had an appointment with Jill Newsome, the Connections Pastor. The receptionist was young and attractive, as was Pastor Newsome, who immediately stepped out from a long corridor of inner offices.

"Call me Jill," the pastor said as she shook Stella's hand, "and welcome to the Renaissance Campus, Stella. We are so glad you have stopped by. Since you are new, I'm going to give you a bit of a tour, and then we'll attend to your business."

"Sounds great," Stella answered. "I'm already intrigued by Renaissance, just in coming through the lounge and the coffee shop."

"We pride ourselves on being the unchurch church, Stella," explained Jill. "We would like to attract people that are successful in life, yet not so much at church. The real go-getters who have felt that traditional church was not keeping up the pace with today's society of global business, technology, and innovation. Some of our regulars even just get coffee and sit in the café watching the church service on the big screen, so they don't have to go into the auditorium. The unchurch worship way, I guess."

"That's …" Stella paused, "… interesting."

"Exactly," Jill confirmed. "We want to be the most interesting, inviting, and cool place to be on the weekend."

Moving right along, they were now in the auditorium, all black, no windows, but with an enormous stage, state-of-the-art lighting, a cutting-edge sound system, and giant screens that flanked the stage on both sides. The audience seating was rows and rows of padded folding chairs that could be removed and/or rearranged for different types of events. At this point, the band had dispersed for a break, so the two women visited about Renaissance. High up in the back of the auditorium, just below the ceiling, were the sound and light technician booths positioned behind glass. On each side of the stage were cameras with robotic arms, unmanned now but ready for the next event.

"We livestream all events here over the internet, broadcast on our website," Jill explained, describing their use of technology. "Online church is here. Many of our active members first came to church via the internet, watching us from home or wherever they were, online. They were able to try us out and see if this is church for them. Then, they find their way here and that's when I meet them."

"Connections?" Stella asked.

"Yes, our goal is to introduce ourselves to people through networks (virtual or social), interest them in coming here, meet them during their visit, make a connection, get them engaged, and then crown that with a commitment to our church covenant," Jill expounded on the process.

"Like a signed document?" Stella asked, somewhat surprised.

"Yes, with a commitment of involvement and supporting God's work here as the evidence of their personal spiritual formation. We are a team, Stella. Our church is *teamwork*," Jill emphasized the last word.

"Oh, that's nice, Jill," Stella responded, not knowing what to say.

"We are not called by Jesus Christ to be consumers. We are called to be disciples. Just as we exude discipline in our business and personal life for success, we can likewise commit to our Lord Jesus at church. Faithful disciples of Christ are fully committed to the enterprise of his church, Stella."

"Committed to Jesus, yes, and to his church as gifted by the Holy Spirit. However, I don't see a signed church covenant as a church model in the Bible, Jill," Stella commented. "I also don't see quotas for financial commitment and time commitment. However, thank you for explaining what you are about here, and showing me your magnificent facility, Jill. I appreciate it."

"You're welcome, Stella," Jill said as the two ladies left the auditorium and took seats in the lounge or salon area by the waterfalls. "Now, how can I help you today, Stella? You said you had a question."

"Yes, Jill. Since you are the Connections Pastor, I wondered if you knew of a young lady named Jade Johnson, who I heard had attended your church, Renaissance, from time to time."

"She was a high school student, yes?" Jill asked.

"She was, and then Jade went to Chicago for university studies this fall," Stella said.

"Well, I met her a few times over the past couple of years. However, she was running her own Bible Study for the Cheer Squad outside of church, and we wondered why she didn't become more engaged with the youth group here," Jill noted.

"The Cheer Squad have said there were some issues with the Youth Pastor, Jason Wheeler, the last couple of years. He was attractive with the latest clothes and haircut, however, the teens felt he was trying to be more of a pal or companion than a role model. They, at least that group of girls, were not comfortable with him," Stella explained.

"I wish we would have been notified of this earlier, before Jade went off to the university," Jill said thoughtfully.

"Oh, the girls did speak up about it, but they felt they weren't believed, so they dropped the issue," Stella relayed. "That's when their Bible Study moved to meeting at Sven & Wong's restaurant on Saturday mornings. Dave Swenson and Lily Wong's daughter, Julie, was part of the group. So, Dave and Lily became Dad and Mom for the group and served them breakfast on Saturdays during their Bible Study."

"Jason Wheeler, our Youth Pastor, is an incredibly cool dude. He is very popular, especially with the girls," Jill said with pride.

"I know that, Jill, and that's why this group was not interested in the youth activities at your church," Stella said. "Although they attended worship, they set up boundaries to distance themselves from Jason and stayed away."

"That's crazy!" Jill said. "He's a great guy!"

"Well, this group of girls, in their quest to be godly, saw otherwise. This leads me to my other question, but I think you've already answer it, Jill," Stella said.

"What question is that?" Jill asked.

"I was going to ask if you know if Jason has surreptitiously been pursuing any of the church girls. He is married and, in his late thirties, although he tried to act young and be attractive to the teens – skinny jeans, plaid shirts, gooped up hair. Yet, I now know better than to ask, since you were unaware of this 'cool dude's' proclivity for the teen girls," Stella admitted.

"There's no point in asking," Stella went on. "However, if I were you, Jill, I'd take a closer look at how Jason is interacting with the young ladies in the youth program," Stella advised.

"Jason's record is clean," Jill insisted. "I don't know what in the world you are talking about."

"A record is clean until the truth is uncovered, if indeed, there is an underlying, contradictory truth," Stella pointed out. "In any case, talk to the girls in your youth program. They have said they know things. Try listening, taking a second look, believing them. It might save your program in the end. Some churches are now faced with lawsuits for not paying attention. Can't imagine what some will face in heaven someday. It doesn't go away."

At this point, Pastor Jill lost interest. She said, "I hope you and your family will come and visit Renaissance and see our band in action on a Saturday night or a Sunday morning. We also have an entertaining children's program for your kids while you and your husband are here. We keep them occupied and entertained for you."

The waterfalls murmured softly in the background.

Stella answered by extending her hand and saying, "Thanks so much for your time today, Jill. I appreciate it."

As Stella walked out the front door of the big black box church to her car parked in the lot, she could hear the band playing again, after their coffee break. Stella looked at the bright clean clear sky and took a deep breath as she got into her car. She wasn't any closer to the truth she was seeking, or, was she?

* * *

Chapter Eighteen
Bonfire and *Out from the Jaws of the Dragon 7: Growing Up*

(Bonfire Books began their Friday review of the next three chapters.)

In fifth grade one day, Sophia's class was in line ready to go to lunch, lights out, with the room a subtle and shadowy grey. In the twilight nothing appeared sharply, but some things were revealed clearly.

The teacher approached to give directions, stopping beside Sophia and between the two separate rows of boys and girls. A grandmotherly type, the teacher paused, throwing a quick glance at Sophia's pink sweater. From the sweater the teacher peered deep into Sophia's eyes, turned away, and then moved toward the door. The other students had followed the teacher's eyes. The boys giggled while ogling Sophia's soft pink sweater. No undergarments were beneath the sweater.

The teacher frowned disapproval and reprimanded the boys. Looking down at her own chest, Sophia saw the circles, but she did not respond. The boys' stares haunted Sophia's mind, forever. She sank back and slouched. She neither saw nor felt any longer the stares or the circles. In Sophia's mind, with a knife she removed the two dark circles, sending them floating down two rivers of blood. The rivers flowed from the chest, draining it dry. The chest, relieved, and free again, was flat, and no longer needed surveillance. Sophia felt she had failed, and then succeeded.

Sophia hated the circles because they were sensitive, and they stuck out. How could anything sensitive blatantly stand out and expect to get away with it? Promiscuous they were, offering themselves to the world as mountaintops. She hated them. Cut them off, she said. Erase.

God had created woman and then abandoned her. He did not take care of her. Sophia would have given anything to be a man. Protecting her body was something she could not do. She didn't know how. She was terrified.

There came the time in adolescence when womanhood approached Sophia, with a monthly cycle, the arising of a sleeping chest, and nests in private places. Sophia awakened in rage, in fear, in anger, in revolt. It was not a quiet unfolding that she felt but a terrifying invasion and she protested and screamed inside; but there was no sound. It was the mind refusing the body, declaring that this could not go forward. It was not safe and only beckoned trouble. This woman was not meant to be. She felt men would come after her for sure now, in her bed, under the sheets, beneath her clothes. They would come to witness the entire event of womanhood, and she would be plundered to become their instrument, their tool. She felt within herself the creation of a being for them, not for herself and her life, but for their lusts and violence, their evil. She was to magnetically draw their evil and connect with it in who she was. Her dad, Mr. Lewis, would find her, her a vessel, he to fill the vessel. Sophia protested. God, NO, she screamed, she pleaded, she begged. It seemed God did not hear her cry; the monthly anguish, thunderous pain and floods of blood came. She refused the woman. Yet the woman found her.

As Sophia matured, when the Lewis family received boxes of secondhand clothes, she would have to try on and model them in front of Mr. Lewis. He said he wanted to help Sophia put together a suitable wardrobe. Sophia's body would cringe together tight and stiff until she could mentally negate feelings, ignoring his glances, while going through the motions of putting on the clothes. She would have to parade before him as if on a catwalk, turning around while he directed her. One night, Mr. and Mrs. Lewis argued loudly about this procedure of modeling. Mrs. Lewis came out against it, criticizing Mr. Lewis' attention.

Mr. Lewis' hands were ready to grab what he saw. As Sophia matured, she slouched her shoulders to hide her developing figure, over her mother's admonitions to "Straighten up!" Desperate, ashamed, and frightened, Sophia could not bear exposure, with her father's increasing sexual advances ever threatening. Home was being a piece of meat in a cage with a hungry wolf. Sophia was always on guard; there was no rest.

Closeness meant sex. Any intimacy, any yearning for love or affection from Mr. Lewis was interpreted as sexual invitation and he responded by violating the object with his insatiable desires. One could pretend he was normal and imagine that the sexual part didn't exist. The world, and certainly the church, didn't seem to think there was anything wrong. He was approved and sanctioned by them. Then he came in the night.

The girl entered womanhood with a numb body, refusing to acknowledge physical existence. Growing up came and went, repressed. But if what her body experienced was not under her control, her mind became her own, bypassing body changes altogether. She was to keep mind and body separate, not allowing one to know what the other was doing, out of fear and self-preservation. In her mind, the girl tried to preserve innocence, dignity, and self-respect. It worked until mind and body communicated with each other. Then she felt dirtied by a strange monster of a man – an animal prowling, pawing, licking, slobbering. Her body was a dumping ground for everything the monster man dished out, depending on the man's needs at the time. What remained, she felt, was a garbage heap: repugnant, stinking, decayed.

"Hey, Ugly," Mark would address the girl. She believed the description, at times, doubting herself. She felt with those words, that Mark at least had finally talked to her. Maybe he was right? She didn't get the good genes? Maybe her appearance was ugly. She had stopped looking in the mirror. "Ugly" was the identity her biological family wanted to imprint on her insides.

Bethany Lewis, her mother, insisted that Sophia looked like Mr. Lewis, her dad. Mrs. Lewis then pointed out the aged relatives of the Lewis extended family, predicting that this was how Sophia would look after her teen years. Their hair was white, and Sophia's hair was a deep auburn. But Mrs. Lewis said that at age twenty, her daughter's hair would suddenly lose color and turn grey, and finally white. Mrs. Lewis also said that about the same time, Sophia would be severely obese with grossly swelled legs, dysfunctional hips, and then lose her mobility. Disabled and elderly at twenty, ending in a premature death, would be Sophia's destiny. Mrs. Lewis claimed that Sophia would get through her teens, barely, but then the death clock would start ticking.

"Life will stop for you at age twenty, just like it did for me, Sophia," Mrs. Lewis declared. "However, unlike me, you will have serious problems with your body."

Sophia pictured herself as middle-aged in her teens. Over her hung a black cloud of insecurity about her body, which seemed to be a prison of filth, disease, and an upcoming premature death. She knew she would soon die.

According to Mrs. Lewis, Sophia looked like her dad, did not belong to her mother, and like Mr. Lewis, Sophia had ruined the life of Mrs. Lewis. The girl was obese, stupid, ugly, dirty, and perverted like Mr. Lewis, her mother claimed. The girl was not a woman. Not a man. She was a thing, an it, a perversion.

On a warm spring evening, almost at sunset, Sophia embarked on what seemed an endless trek, the mile from school to home. Distraught, the girl brain-directed her steps without feeling. Go, walk. Her heart was trailing in the street dust behind, tears wanted to come but crying had long been abandoned for self-control and determination. This night, she dragged herself homeward.

Sophia was a star at school. An outstanding student, she had been cited as talented. There was almost nothing Sophia could not do well at school. Awards were regular occurrences. Without great effort, almost unaware, she was successful. However accomplished, though, as a girl, she lived in a vacuum: a dark, empty tunnel alone, distant from anyone, anything, including, sometimes, herself.

At home, Mr. and Mrs. Lewis demanded perfection from Sophia for their purposes, for hard work in their household.

Sophia was good for nothing until proven good for something. As a result of Sophia's work habits and accomplishments, to those outside the family, she was a showcase. Among family members, however, she drew only disdain.

Returning from awards night, questions and confusion drummed Sophia's mind. If she did not do what her parents expected of her, the girl was overtly punished. Then, as she obeyed, Sophia was covertly hated, even as she followed orders. Where was the third option that would finally open up their arms to lovingly receive her? What was she doing wrong? Would she ever be able to do right? Yes, she would try. Anything. Just love me, please, Sophia's insides implored. Accept me, too, as one who belongs in this family, who is meant to be. Please, she implored a silent plea. But it hurt to keep trying.

Halfway home, waiting at a busy intersection to cross the street, Sophia found her answer for the hurt – it would not matter. She would not hurt. At that moment, the girl disconnected feeling. She lied. She lied to herself and decided to lie to home and to everyone. Sophia's teeth were gritted together, grinding, and she was stiff-lipped. No tears. No sorrow. She could do all, still be mocked, and would not feel it. It wouldn't matter how her family treated her, she decided.

Crossing the street marked the step into the lie. On the other side she couldn't feel the heaviness. From Sophia's lips came songs, and Sophia's legs started skipping. Disconnected, she could see herself singing and tapping out rhythms, smiling, refusing inner feeling. It had been a shameful hurt.

At home, Mr. Lewis had not yet returned from work, or wherever he was. Mrs. Lewis was screaming at the other children. They were racing around the house. Sophia smiled to show her mother that she was not upset, which made Mrs. Lewis even more angry. Sophia then rushed to put the house in order. Sophia vowed that she would find a way to please her mom, and she would not tell her mom about her own hurt feelings. Never. The girl was fearful that she might make her mother feel guilty, and then enraged. Sophia wanted her mother to love her.

As an adult, the woman wrote about what had happened when a little girl was growing up in search of love, particularly from her family.

Whenever the hurt came, the girl continued to lie and leave, so she could go on accomplishing without acknowledging that no one cared, that it didn't matter anyway. Feelings hidden, the girl would work to find love any way possible. When she was mistreated it didn't matter. The girl needed love at any cost.

She felt her gifts and abilities were for taking all the household responsibilities and assuring the parents' marriage didn't fall apart. She was to serve big meals to the Lewis family church friends because, "that girl is talented in the kitchen," they said. "Oh, and she can take care of visiting children because, that girl is good with kids," they added. "By the way, she can do all of the housework because this one is so organized and such a good girl," they continued. The good girl was good in bed with her dad.

Different they labeled her. Different meant able to do everything better than everyone else so doing everything for everyone else. Different was a word that the girl hated. Selected, chosen, gifted, and set apart for every task and whim and desire.

Different meant pretending to be like everyone else but never belonging.

She was born not to be loved, not lovable, not their fault, they could not, should not. Love was not a definitive part of her being. There was no category in this girl for love. She didn't miss it, didn't know it, couldn't feel it. The little girl grew up quietly. She did not rebel, she did not complain, she complied. Her heart was blank or not even present at all. How can one miss what one does not know?

The child could not understand why her mom wouldn't buy her clothes, warm hat and mittens, boots, a winter coat.

She couldn't understand why her life was vastly different from other children. Why couldn't she go out and play, participate in the neighborhood and find friends? What was wrong with her, she questioned. Ugly, dumb, shameful, abilities, her curse but at least she could work so she had to be useful by doing the work. She tried to be good, to earn the opportunity to go out and play. No matter how much she tried, work always overtook, endlessly.

People who had gifts and abilities should not be loved, her mom said, because they may turn out to be arrogant. Enslave them, hold them captive for humility, keep the girl in her place of shame, her mother's way.

People who have gifts and abilities should not be loved, her dad said, because they may turn out to be willful, which is evil and sinful. They should be humiliated, imprisoned, and subjugated by the blade and the belt. Don't let them go. Don't let them loose. Loose ones are free from the knife. Free to roam this earth and be whores. Submission was his requirement for the girl. A girl had to be controlled by her father, so she wasn't dominated by her sin. He was committed to keeping the girl from being a loose woman of the streets. He, manly and powerful, would conquer the beast in the little girl.

The girl was told she had gifts and abilities, so she should not be loved, but should be controlled. It would behoove the girl to give and not to take, to lay down her life, to sacrifice for others that she might flee sin and arrogance.

When the girl cried, the mother said, "Cry, bawl baby."

When the girl cried, the father said, "I'll give you something to cry about," and he did it all the more.

Chapter Nineteen
Bonfire and *Out from the Jaws of the Dragon 8: Family Doctor*

(The Bonfire Books group continued their Friday dialogue, discussing medical doctors who take advantage of and violate children under their care.)

Approaching adolescence, Sophia experienced excruciatingly sharp monthly cramps. Unaware of a woman's cycle, and generally inattentive to her body, Sophia became frightened at the persistence of a pain that she could not always successfully deaden. She entreated her mother to take her to the Lewis family physician, a noted Christian doctor from their church, and in the area. Weary of her daughter's complaints, Mrs. Lewis finally agreed that Sophia should go.

After getting ready, it was evident that Mr. Lewis, her father, and not Mrs. Lewis, her mom, was going to take Sophia to the doctor for an afterhours appointment, alone. The girl's heart sank. Major regret washed over her. If only she hadn't asked to go in the first place; but the girl could say nothing. The decision had been made.

At the doctor's office, Mr. Lewis sat right there in the acutely cramped patient examination room to which Sophia was assigned. The doctor entered and had the girl undress from the waist down in front of the two grown Christian church-going men. Eventually the physician threw a sheet over Sophia's torso, after she had undressed, and after she was on the table, waiting without her clothes.

The doctor proceeded to examine the girl, inside and out, below the waist, her feminine parts. He asked about the pain. The physician conversed with Mr. Lewis, too, fully describing what he was doing, private parts and all, explaining the particulars of this young girl's development and attributes.

Sophia held still on the table in hushed humiliation, frozen in her feelings, eventually blanking out what was happening. She stared at the ceiling, counting dots and squares. She was no longer a conscious participant. The girl knew what would happen when Mr. Lewis and his daughter got to the car after the appointment. On the way home, Mr. Lewis would want to hold Sophia's hands, stroke her, and have his own discussion with his daughter regarding what the doctor was describing and touching. Mr. Lewis would fondle and kiss. In silent anguish, Sophia blamed herself for precipitating the situation. It was her fault. She had asked for it.

One evening in the master bedroom, Mr. Lewis and Sophia were on the floor, carpet royal blue, door ajar, talking about little things. He said he needed to get to know his daughter who was growing up quickly, already almost a teen. Did Sophia want to be there? She didn't know. There was no "I want". The two were side-by-side, looking at the ceiling, the man posing questions about school, the girl striving to answer correctly, seeking to be a good girl, hungering to love and be loved. The girl's feelings – Mr. Lewis wanted to know how she felt about growing up. Sophia told her dad that she needed more independence and more privacy - a girl her age.

"Of course," Mr. Lewis whispered softly. Then he pulled the girl up, face-to-face on top of him, beginning his routine. When Sophia pulled away, he said he was her father, getting to know his daughter. The girl did not respond, but the man continued to question and continued. The girl could keep talking about her feelings and feel nothing. The man did not take her clothes off yet. He would do so later in the girl's bed in the dark.

In the wee hours of the night, house pitch black, the Lewis family was in the middle of sleep. Sophia's bedroom was on the second level of the two-story Tudor home, past the bathroom and off to one corner at the end of the hallway. From down the hallway, Sophia could hear the rhythm of Mark snoring down the hall. The girl was not awake, not asleep. Mr. Lewis, fully clothed, led the girl's exposed body down the hall, into the bathroom. The man washed the girl off like he used to when she was very small, only she was no longer a little girl. He despised the smells, the girl's filth.

Chapter Twenty
Bonfire and *Out from the Jaws of the Dragon 9: A Grey Day*

(The Bonfire group continued their Friday dialogue with reflection about adults who overpower children and hide in plain sight in a community. The novella had evoked startling images.)

It was one those grey days when the weather doesn't make you feel anything. Not cold, not hot, not bright, not dark: dull, void, nothing. Grey sky over them, grey highway under them - somehow nothing was to be notable and Sophia was not to remember this day. But she did remember; beneath the placid surroundings, personal violence was taking place. Another stripping-down and ravaging of privacy and personal wholeness. Another scream so great her lungs would not release it.

How Mr. and Mrs. Lewis made the decision, Sophia did not know, but she remembered that the two parents discussed and agreed together. Without the rest of the family, Mr. Lewis and Sophia were alone in the car, on the way to their family church for a sex education class.

"Oh Mom, please," Sophia had begged, "Why?" In the end, however, Sophia decided it was better to go along than risk their wrath.

In the car, sitting in her mom's seat, every ounce of Sophia's energy was focused on not experiencing anything. Sophia denied hearing, seeing, feeling, any sensual input. Her energy was not great enough. Words, a voice, and a hand seeped through.

There was something agonizing about the story Mr. Lewis was telling his daughter, even though the words made no sense at all. Two people were on a plane traversing the country, a man and a woman, side-by-side. The woman told the man she carried joy bags in her purse. Yes, she showed him, she had joy bags. It was the word, joy bags. Bags? Baggies? The way Mr. Lewis told the story, and the way he stroked his daughter's hand, Sophia knew there was something else going on. Pulling the plug on feeling in her hand, arm, and shoulder, Sophia felt dominated and invaded without knowing why. Sophia stared out the window, away from Mr. Lewis, muttering, "Oh," not daring to move away from him. Any response, positive or negative, always seemed to entice the man.

At church, the event leaders separated the two from the Lewis family; Mr. Lewis went with the other dads and their sons. Sophia was directed to follow the mothers and daughters to an auditorium with a screen and rows of metal folding chairs. Together they watched a video explaining girls' adolescent development.

Alone. All the other girls were with their mothers. One mother stared deep and long into Sophia's eyes, boring a whole right through her to the floor. Sophia could feel her words, accusing her of luring her father into bringing his daughter to a sex education film with him, "You little whore."

Sophia sat by herself in a corner, trying not to take in anything going on around her. Somehow Sophia did mentally record the screening, the story of a mother and daughter at the time the daughter was beginning her womanhood cycle. From Sophia's vantage point, the film should have had subtitles; it was foreign. Mrs. Lewis had never helped her daughter understand anything about a woman's body, development, a woman's cycle, or hygiene.

When the lights came on, questions and discussion followed. Soon Mr. Lewis joined the women's group and talked with the ladies, flirting with the younger ones. Sophia held her corner, waiting for Mr. Lewis to finish networking with the church women and their daughters.

Going home was in the dark so Sophia couldn't see anything, but she knew Mr. Lewis was aroused. Once again, he had made the girl's body and her feelings his business. He had won - he had his way - even the church had seemed to cooperate. Sophia had been made to submit, to turn over control completely to him until he could sense no restraint. That was his endeavor, his success, the way he wanted it to be. He would visit his daughter later that night in her room.

As a grown-up woman, Sophia realized that during her entire childhood and growing up, Mr. Lewis worked on arousing sexual feelings in his daughter. As a child even, she was repulsed, she hated herself, she hated him, she hated being a woman, she feared men, she hated sexuality, she hated feeling, she hated being. Numb. Then, Mr. Lewis forced his way. He did as he pleased. He was the dad – father – bestowed with power, granted by the church, by her mother, by the extended family, by the society she knew. Power appointed to him by power from above, the very Creator, God. Mr. Lewis was god.

Sophia was in bed at night. Thick darkness filled the cold walls of her room. On the bed sheet, under the comforter, stuffy hot skin was cemented together. It was crowded in bed with Mr. Lewis. Sweaty, body to body, enclosed together, imprisoned. He was holding his daughter, he in her, her body holding him. When the girl protested, the man summoned God. He was connected to God. Sophia to him, he to God. Mr. Lewis said there was no choice. A father had no choice, God wanted it that way.

It was something the girl never wanted to talk about. It was too painful for her and as a child, not quite a woman, she did not have the right words to describe what was happening. But she knew the pain. Powerless to separate herself from the pain, she separated within herself, as the body of the girl and the brain of the girl. She recorded what was happening, but she tried to feel nothing.

The body was screaming, "No, no, no, don't."

The brain was numbing, "It doesn't matter, you cannot feel it."

The body, "Keep the legs together, please don't let the monster man pull them apart."

The brain, "The legs will fall wide open, flat, straddled. Never mind, it is none of your business. Be still to let this pass."

The body, "Don't let him cut me open, don't let him tear me apart. Don't let him put in the knife."

The brain, "The place is a void anyway. You can feel nothing."

The body, "I'm tearing apart, it's bleeding, help! It's shredding me apart, help me someone, please!"

The brain, "Be quiet and be a good girl. Respect your elders, be a nice daughter, submissive, calm, serene, winsome, and content. You are destroying your chance of being a good Christian daughter. Silence will save you. The silence and submission of a girl is what pleases God."

The girl was numb.

It always hurt when the knife went in, though. Sophia did not move, or the knife would cut her insides and tear her even more. She was placid still. Frozen, no sound. Passage screaming. Pain. Cut open where there was no opening before. A violation forced through a closed door. There was no movement in her body. She did not know what was happening except she did not dare move. She did not pull away or his force would become greater. She did not go forward, or the knife would go deeper, shredding, stabbing inside her. She blacked it out. She numbed it out. She was only to be present like a brick. It was her obligation. She had to hold the knife inside between her legs. Taking part was her job – being there. It was numb presence. Tormented numb presence. It was agony.

What the man was doing was not for the girl to know. It was none of her business. She was to ignore, forget, erase, and simply let it happen. He ripped apart her legs and put himself in between. Her legs howled. Her in-between howled. Then silence. He was busy. The girl was gone.

It did not matter, she told herself. She would learn to use knives also and cut out all of the pain. She would chop the girl up, too, and her screaming would be silenced. She would not have to listen to the body screaming any more. The doctors had thought the girl had played with herself. No, she did not touch. The body was not hers to touch. The girl's body belonged to him. She would get rid of that body, and that would get rid of him, too. She would cut free – cut loose from her body, from the monster man, once and for all. He could have the body, but not her mind, and not her soul.

In bed, Sophia could feel Mr. Lewis hotly, and then she could not feel him. She switched it off. No feeling, no presence. Numb to self, to the monster man, to God. But her mind was ticking, awake, recording all. She could not sleep. She closed her eyes, but the man was still there, and God was there, holding them together, the man said. The man would pour in the lifeblood, the life breath, the life fluids. Life from God, to the man, to the girl. Let there be life, God had said, and the girl opened up her eyes and looked up. God was above, she thought, over the bed, authorizing the man who was holding the girl. God was watching. God's eyes surveying. God's presence a vigil. The girl tried to speak to God, but God was nodding, "Yes, good, and faithful servant. Good girl." Mr. Lewis said, "Good girl," too.

Sophia told herself that she was a good girl, and that's what she wanted to be.

Later, alone, in her mind, Sophia hated her body for being attractive to the man, for being so good. In her silence and with the body still feeling the presence of what the man had done, Sophia, still a girl and not quite a woman, came up with a plan in her mind to destroy the goodness. In her mind, she imagined going to the kitchen to find the biggest, sharpest chopping knife. It had a shiny, cold blade. In her thoughts, Sophia put on a white butcher's apron and then placed the body soiled by the monster man on a white metal table. She thought of chopping up the body with concise, clean cuts.

There was no blood dripping. In her imagination, the body was frozen numb. There was no pain either. She imagined cutting through the bones quickly while the out-cold body was switched off to feeling. From the feet (two slices), she imagined moving to the legs and spacing each thrust of the blade evenly, about five inches apart. She thought to wrap each chunk neatly in white butcher paper, sealing the package with a fat hunk of masking tape, and labelling it with a black marker. Each wrapped piece, she imagined, would be stacked into a freezer. At last when the body had been completely segmented and put away, she felt that her mind could rest at ease. The girl had been put to rest. The man was not there, and he would not have to come back.

What terrorized the girl? His presence in darkness, the knife in the shadows, hands that wandered, lips that smothered, touching skin, the taste was bitter, feeling his power, she could not see him.

She said, "No."

He said, "God."

* * *

164

Chapter Twenty-One
Jake & Stella: Amazed

Friday, October 19th, 8:15 p.m., Jake texted Stella: Fire in firepit. Moon above.

Stella was ready for a crackling fire and moonlit autumn night when she pulled up to the cabin in the woods along the river. The Alpine Bed and Breakfast lodging had auxiliary cabins for rent on the grounds, among pines and other woodsy flora. Jake had reserved a rustic cabin for a nature night with his beloved. Earlier that evening, Jake had dropped off the children with Grandpa Jack and Grandma Sara, after their Daddy outing and dinner. Arriving ahead of Stella, Jake checked in, threw his backpack into the cabin, lit up the fire, unwound, and waited. He didn't have to wait long.

After parking her car, Stella walked up to the cabin with her overnight bag and took in a deep breath of cool autumn air. This was perfect. She tossed her shoulder bag in the cabin alongside Jake's backpack, and then joined him under the night sky, at the campfire.

Jake had positioned two outdoor recliners to face the fire, covering them each with a couple of fleece blankets to roll up in for retaining body warmth in the cool night air. A small table had two wine stems and a bottle of red. As Stella settled into a chaise, Jake reached over, then she leaned forward a bit, and Jake gave her a back massage. She sighed with relaxation and relief.

"Friday night with you, Jake. I'll take it," Stella whispered. It was going to be a wonderful night.

As Jake massaged her spine all the way up to the back of her neck, he reached the base of her head. "Now, you can tell me what's going on in that lovely head of yours, dear Stella," he said.

"Well, if you really want to know..." she began.

"I do, my love," Jake interrupted.

"I was thinking about that TED Talk that former President Jimmy Carter gave a number of years ago, 2015 maybe?" Stella said thoughtfully.

"And...?" Jake asked.

"He said that the number one human rights abuse in the world is the mistreatment of women and girls," Stella recalled.

"No question about that," Jake agreed.

"He elaborated with many examples, that supported three reasons for this mistreatment: first, the misinterpretation of religious teaching among a variety of religions, where leaders consign women to a secondary position to men in the eyes of God," Stella articulated.

"Unfortunately, I heard some of that this week with regard to women being able to even lead a women's Bible Study on their own. It doesn't seem right. It doesn't really come from the Bible, and there are those, like The Junia Project, for one, that argue from the Bible the case for women's equality with men," Jake contributed. "Now what's the second reason for this subservience?" he asked.

"A second contribution to this problem of the abuse of women and girls is the increasing prevalence in the world of resorting to violence. Women are already deemed to be secondary in the eyes of God, so women and girls end up vulnerable and at the receiving end of much of this violence," Stella said solemnly. "It's serious, it's cruel, it's heart-rending."

"And we are raising a son and a daughter, Stella. This is something to consider in regard to parenting. That our son respect girls, and our daughter be respected in all of the avenues of her life – school, work, relationships, society," Jake added. "And what is the third issue that contributes to this problem?" Jake queried.

"You segued right into the third issue, my dear. Carter said that the problem is that many men don't really care about these issues. 'Don't give a damn' is what he said, as I recall. We need to raise our son to care about equality with women – even better, about quality of life for women, and to not apathetically ride out his life without active empathy," Stella noted. "I'm so thankful I married a guy who really does care – love you, Jake."

"Love you, too, Stella," Jake said. "After all of my failures with women and being brought to my knees about my selfishness and pride, God saved me from myself, and brought me you, Stella. It just puts evidence to the fact that we really do have a saving Christ, and a loving and forgiving God," Jake confessed.

"We do. A blessing for both of us, love," Stella looked him in the eyes, then cupped the palm of her hand under his chin and held him tenderly.

"Do you think about what could have happened to Jade Johnson in Chicago?" Jake asked.

"All the time," Stella answered. "It seems that the church was not a big help this week. Apparently, she's not their demographic. She's not what they were looking for in their ministries."

"For sure," Jake said. "It's odd, though, because the lost sheep that Jesus said the shepherd rescued was just – a sheep. Nothing special. And with the Good Samaritan, again, I don't know if demographics played into it. There was just someone there plundered by the side of the road that needed help."

"At our book club, in the novella we are reading, we're witnessing a hypothetical story, a parable of sorts, about a girl being tossed to the side of the road with the usual suspects just passing her by. They turn their backs on her suffering. Brutal," Stella declared, "and completely merciless."

"Yeah, how is that going?" Jake asked.

"The story is getting more intense, worse, really," Stella said. "But it is revealing what goes on in the subcurrent or subtext of our prim and proper Christian society. Not a pretty picture. Though it is fiction, these stories are in the news every week, it seems."

"In the story, will that girl end up like Jade Johnson, do you think?" asked Jake.

"No, the novella opens with her assurance that Jesus is her Shepherd and he rescued her, eventually," Stella answered. "It's amazing, really, because…"

Just then they were interrupted by a phone call on Jake's cell. He looked at the caller's name, answered, and quickly put on speaker phone, "Yes, Richard, what do you have for us?"

"Stella and Jake, you are not going to believe this," Richard said right away. "I'm in touch with one of the detectives. He will be coming out to Sunnyside soon to do interviews. He'll want to talk with you two, for sure. As it turns out, your incredible college student had security cameras hidden behind the plants in her apartment. They have a complete record of what came down in that place. She was one brilliant student. She knew what she was doing."

"Why in the world would she think to put cameras on the inside of her apartment?" Stella thought out loud.

"There's some kind of work that she was engaged in to support herself. Her job. She was doing some kind of business in her place. Paperwork on the dining room table. Businessmen coming and going. We'll be in touch, but don't be surprised when the Chicago detectives show up in your town looking for interviews and seeking information. Jade Johnson video recorded everything that went on in her place, and they just have to figure out who is who and what is what. This student solved her own case."

"Amazing," Jake and Stella replied together, looking at each with great surprise.

Then they heard a "Click", indicating that the phone call had ended.

PART IV

Chapter Twenty-Two
Cowboy Dad

Monday, October 22nd, 8:45 a.m., Jake texted Stella: Breakfast with Dad, our Cowboy.

Jake was in the Cowboy Supper Club kitchen sipping a mug of steaming hot black coffee with his eyes on his father-in-law who was flipping their eggs, hash browns, smoked beef bratwursts, and toast, on the restaurant kitchen's grill. Jack liked to do it all on the grill, yes, even the toast, and Jake didn't mind watching. Once a month, at least, Jake met with his father-in-law on a Monday morning for breakfast in the Club's kitchen, after the earlier Chamber meeting at Sven and Wong's Family Restaurant was over, and before the Monday help showed up and the day began at Cowboy Jack's. But the real reason Jake was motivated to share breakfast with his father-in-law was to glean from a great father, wonderful husband and a proven community leader, wisdom and encouragement. Cowboy Jack was generous with both wisdom and praise. Jake highly valued his time alone with Stella's dad and their guy talks. This was clearly a bonus for Jake in marrying the lovely Stella. Husband Jake and father Jack had an admirable relationship. It was all good.

"How could we be so lucky, in our little corner of the world, to score a Big Shot like HR Wellington?" Jake pronounced as the two men began their guy breakfast at the Rancher's Table together in earnest. "It's only been a little over a year. HR grew the internship program, and he is now bringing us our very own town podcast, which will eventually become a video channel. So much growth and innovation."

"I'm not impressed," Jack replied quietly. "What does HR stand for, anyway? Harvard Ross? Even the name hints at presumption. Did he actually go to Harvard or is this just some cute Ivy League nickname he gave himself to impress the Midwest rubes?"

"We have a leader here to bring us all into a new place as a community, Jack," Jake stated to his father-in-law.

"At what cost there, my dear boy?" the Cowboy scrutinized.

"What do you mean, 'at what cost'?" Jake asked, thoughtfully.

"I mean that when someone just blows into town with his business, after hip-hopping all over the countryside in the course of his career, and then sets himself up, immediately, as the number one business guy in the community, the president of the Chamber of Commerce, don't you question the motives, Jake?" Jack asked.

"He seems to want to develop Sunnyside, to put us on the map," Jake answered.

"Sunnyside is already on the map, due to the history of our community patriarchs, and matriarchs. Don't forget about the women," the dad asserted. "Back in the day, there were the settlers, the farmers, the lumber barons, and the factory developers. The railroad and the highways and the river connected everyone here with the nation-at-large for trade. Later, the airport and higher education were added. Now, through technology, we are virtually connected all over the world. This all happened long before Mr. Harvard showed up. You've got it backwards, Jake. That guy came to this county to catch the wave for himself, the wave of what was already going on here, in this rather ideal community, even if I do say so, myself."

"What's wrong with that?" asked Jake. "He saw a good thing and he is going to join and build."

"Nothing wrong with joining and building," Jack admitted. "But do you even notice how he operates? When he is in the room, all eyes are on him. He rules. He has his say and then he has his way. I wonder how long this is going to last. It's problematic. We are not a town of sycophants, in my view – though Mr. Harvard may think we are. Which is why you don't always see me at the Chamber of Commerce meetings. I would like to keep a distance for a spell to see what this man is really up to. He has increasingly put himself in a position of power and control, of running the show. It looks noble and altruistic, however, there may be something afoot that has a sinister underbelly. I, for one, am not convinced that his motives are clear and pure," the elder man added.

Jack then asked his son-in-law a critical question, "Is this about dominate, control, and manipulate – once he is in position?"

After a pause, Jack rephrased his own question with, "Or, is this truly about serving, collaboration, and respect? That's what you have to become aware of, Jake. What's the real game plan here?"

"I guess I never question motives," the younger Jake, admitted. "If it looks good, I go with it."

"Well, then you have something to learn," the father-in-law advised. "The problem with this Harvard fellow is not just that he attracts attention or catches the eye. It seems like he has an enormous need to stand out from the pack. Self-aggrandizement, one-upmanship, and status above others seem to be his focus. No tower is high enough for him. The need is insatiable, to build his own dynasty, at the cost of others, and on the backs of others – their efforts, not his - mind you."

"What about Mrs. Wellington, Daisy, his wife?" Jake asked.

"That's a good question," the Cowboy acknowledged. "Is the missus also a narcissist? She doesn't seem so. However, I put money on it that when Daisy married Harvard Ross, she didn't have a clue, either. He probably wined and dined her, made her feel like a queen – for a day though, so to speak. Good Christian pillar of the community he was. Still is, as a matter of fact, yet short of humility. Once she got hitched, she simply continues to go along for the ride. The roller coaster ride with a person who has an ego that is like a black hole."

"That sounds devastating," Jake remarked.

"It is," Jack said. "However, I don't believe she is helpless. There are avenues in our society to deal with a failed relationship. You and Stella are lawyers, Jake. You understand this better than anyone in our culture. It's not easy for a woman being married to a narcissist, but there are ways to explore other options. Maybe she has, maybe she hasn't. Maybe she enjoys the benefits of his wealth and celebrity. Certainly, she cannot enjoy all the moving around they have done over the years."

"I wonder how she feels about their former intern, Jade Johnson?" Jake asked.

"Now, you're thinking, Son. Have you spoken with Daisy about Jade?" the Cowboy answered the question with a question.

"No, we haven't done that yet. I spoke with HR a week ago at the Monday Chamber of Commerce meeting, and he couldn't get away from me quick enough. Then, this morning, he avoided me altogether. I left instead of waiting around for him. I doubt he would have wanted to spend the time to talk anyway. He seems to be avoiding me," Jake observed.

"That's it! No empathy. He knows you and Stella have been asking about Jade Johnson. News travels fast in this town. Here HR's former intern ran into some kind of trouble, deadly trouble, in Chicago and her former boss is indifferent. That's wrong, just plain wrong. See what I mean, Jake? Doesn't that seem wrong to you?" Jack asked.

"I thought he was just busy," Jake admitted.

"Too busy? A situation regarding the girl who began her career in his office, probably working very diligently for very little pay, and he is not interested in her welfare? That's outright cold and heartless," the Cowboy asserted. "There's your proof that there is something wrong with the leadership of Mr. Harvard, and his wife, as she hasn't batted an eyelash either. Doesn't Daisy work in the very same office?"

"She does," Jake affirmed. "He's gone a lot, out with customers and contracts and such. Business trips. Daisy runs the office and keeps everything in order from the home front."

"So, Daisy worked with Jade Johnson, on site," Jack concluded. "And she has not approached you about Jade, has she?"

"No, she hasn't. The Cheer Squad girls are the ones who brought the whole situation to our attention. We've been working with them, first to find out why Jade was not answering their calls, and then to pursue why she was murdered. It's a homicide. A truly shattering situation all around, for everyone," Jake spoke softly but firmly, concerned.

"That says a lot, too. This couple may be new to this town, but they are also of a different variety of character. They just don't care about their fellow human being, someone who gave of her life to them, then had that life taken away. Total disregard for human life," Jack maintained. "Let them never say they are pro-life in my presence. They are not. They are anti-life. Plain and simple."

"That's a bold statement," Jake noted.

"I mean every word of it," Jack confirmed. "HR Wellington is not a leader in this town. He is a parasite. He and his business aspirations are feeding off of the goodness of this town, only to build up his own empire with no regard for innocent human life. That's dead wrong and it is deadly," Jack concluded.

Chapter Twenty-Three
Human Resources

Tuesday, October 23rd, 9:30 a.m., Jake texted Stella: At HR's office suite, waiting.

The receptionist business intern, Lexi, was serving Jake a double espresso in the greeting area when Stella emerged from the elevator to enter the sixth-floor headquarters office suite of HR Wellington. Gold letters identified that this was the HR Wellington floor, as mounted on the side walls of the carved wood and stone archway preceding the spacious welcome expanse. "Human Resource Expertise to Advance your Enterprise" was the tagline that accompanied the business name in smaller but equally bold – and gold - raised mounted lettering. Beyond the reception area were a maze of cubicles, and beyond the workspaces was a wall of windows that faced the morning sunrise over the Mississippi River.

Lexi floated gracefully about, addressing Jake as "Mr. Peltier, Sir," in a gentle, yielding voice, as she handed him his coffee, while displaying long, perfectly manicured nails, soft pale hands, and a smooth approach. Then Lexi progressed to seating Mrs. Peltier after taking her coat, and requesting what she would like for a beverage, too. Stella observed the movements of the intern as she put away her coat and returned with her coffee. Lexi, the intern, was beautifully dressed, trying hard to please, and learning how to interact in a business environment. Obviously, this was her first rodeo, and Lexi was focused on meeting the needs of the customers while aiming to please her boss, too. She seemed quiet, submissive, obedient, polished, polite, poised, refined, naïve, inexperienced, agreeable, responsible, well-turned-out, coifed and manicured, subtly intelligent (the kind of student that gets good grades but never asks a question), and a people-pleaser (maybe, more precisely, a boss-pleaser). For some supervisors, Lexi was the perfect employee.

Stella noted the intern's delicate voice and watched her elegant demeanor, then remarked in a whisper to Jake after Lexi left their area, "I wonder if this would have been Jade Johnson, one year ago."

Stella wanted to talk with Lexi, but the intern was gone, having returned to faithfully hiding in silence, seated behind her desk, attentive to the beck and call of Mr. Harvard Ross Wellington and Mrs. Daisy Layne Wellington, the business owners, President, and Vice President, respectively.

"But what had made Jade different? What got her into trouble in Chicago?" Jake scribbled on a notebook that he had retrieved from his pocket and then showed to Stella. "Lexi seems to be the embodiment of complaisance. She would never rock the boat, so to speak. She would only accommodate, as I imagine Jade would, also. No red flags, there."

It was not as if Jake and Stella were going to let on regarding what was happening with their mission of concern for Jade. They wanted to have a simple visit with HR Wellington himself, while getting a feel for his business, the place where Jade Johnson had last worked before she left for Chicago. Busy with their own family and work affairs, it had been months since the Peltier couple had actually sat down and spoken with HR for a real conversation. As a matter of fact, they had never even had a real conversation with Daisy Wellington, his wife, the VP. Though Vice President and second-in-command, Daisy seemed to operate in the shadows, like a good Christian wife should, some would say.

Over the past month of October, at the Chamber of Commerce meetings, HR had escaped the lawyers' inquiries. Today, however, since HR was in town and in his office, they had set an appointment with the CEO to just visit in his headquarters and discuss human resources. This was HR's enterprise; perhaps the lawyers, as small business owners, could seek human resources services for Legal Grounds.

The business ambience and tempo of the HR Wellington establishment seemed sophisticated, classy, and dignified. Everyone conversed in muted tones and moved about with confidence. The taupe leather couches and easy chairs in the welcome area were top-drawer and comfortable. Original oil paintings of quaint cottages, forests with footpaths, and warm sunsets hung well-placed on the walls, in mock gold frames. The low tables for coffee cups and computers were polished and shiny. The ladies at their desks were all young and attractive and quietly busy working, expressing lovely smiles when they looked up intermittently. Yes, they were all ladies, the employees that they could see from the reception area. Even the air smelled like a spruce forest, clean, fresh and pleasant.

"Perhaps Jade had found relief in working in this well-run business during her senior year at Sunnyside High School," Stella scribbled back a note to Jake on his pocket notepad.

Stella knew from her visits with the Cheer Squad, that Jade's family sure didn't seem empathetic and warm with their oldest daughter, Jade. Indeed, the Cheer Squad had told Stella that each time the Squad had flown in from a Cheer Competition trip, the Squad members and their parents routinely provided Jade with a ride to her family's home from the airport. Once they realized no one from the Johnson home would pick Jade up from the airport, the other girls and their parents stepped in to help their Squad Leader. The Cheer Squad girls had even said that they felt they found out what mean was when they got to know Jade Johnson's family, the worst being her mother and younger sister. However, they felt Jade's brother was unkind also, and that Mr. Johnson ruled his household like an autocrat. Good grief, they were all evil, the Cheer Squad had decided. It was not as if the Johnson family members didn't have issues like in every family, but instead of pulling together, they ripped one another apart, especially Jade. She seemed to be their number one target. Yet, even with this backdrop of horror going on at home, Jade was determined to seek God and to succeed, on her own, if necessary. The Cheer girls said that if Jade wore a game face at school, it seemed she wore a coat of armor at home, a bullet proof vest no less, just to hold her head up and keep going. The Johnsons may have had more than enough money, but love seemed in scarce supply at the Grand Estate on the Great River.

Perhaps the highly cultured Wellingtons had been the perfectly promising parent figures for the young Jade. Perhaps they filled an enormous void, a hidden wound in the life of Jade Johnson, that had helped her navigate away from her cruel family and into a safer, saner place with a more promising future.

Jake and Stella already were familiar with the fact that HR owned a highly regarded human resources agency in their town – cleverly using his "Harvard Ross" to be substituted with Human Resources in the name of his business, HR Wellington.

The corporate name reflected both himself as CEO, and the services of his enterprise. Wellington leased the entire sixth floor of the tower from Cowboy Jack, Stella's dad, the owner of the Wild Mustang Corral, the mall. In addition to being titled as the CEO, HR ran the Chamber, led as the Chairman of the Board of his church, donated big bucks to community projects, and seemed to be everyone's model of an ideal citizen leader. All of this had been accomplished in a relatively short amount of time – in the barely two years since HR and Daisy landed in the idyllic community of Sunnyside.

Stella peered down the hallway, beyond the reception area. She could see the corridor led to the private offices of the suite. Decorating the hallway were HR's photos of himself with people he deemed important to know, obviously: senators, the mayor, corporate owners, county commissioners, law officers, the school superintendent, community organizers, etc.

Soon another fine young lady appeared and introduced herself to the waiting Jake and Stella. "Good morning, Mr. and Mrs. Peltier," she began. "My name is Faith Metz and I am Mr. Wellington's personal administrative assistant. Would you need a refill of your beverages before your meeting with Mr. Wellington?"

Stella looked at Jake and then answered, "So pleased to meet you, Faith. You can call us Stella and Jake. I think we are all set with our coffee."

"Lovely. Then follow me and I will take you to Mr. Wellington's office," Faith replied, and led them down the hallway to the final office, a corner setting at the end of the passageway with floor-to-ceiling windows that encompassed two full walls of the executive office. "Have a seat," Faith added, and motioned the couple to two plush black leather easy chairs set up in front of HR's epic commanding desk.

The CEO had his back to them and was looking out the window from his larger-than-life leather tall-back desk chair. Once they were seated, HR swung around, and greeted them, standing up, and reaching across his desk to shake the right hand of each visitor, beginning with Jake, then following with Stella.

"Good morning, Jake, and lovely Stella, how pleasant it is to meet together on this fine morning," HR began.

"Thank you for meeting with us on short notice, and good morning to you, HR," Jake answered. "We appreciated your hospitality in your welcome center. Indeed, it was a pleasure to be served espresso by your new intern, Lexi."

"She is a great asset to our company," HR agreed. "We highly appreciate the few hours per week she spends here, learning the business while completing her simple office tasks."

"Just curious, HR, is that the position that Jade Johnson held here, before she went to Chicago?" Stella asked.

"It seems you set this appointment to discuss the opportunities to contract some of our human resources services with your business, Jake," HR said with an air of control, and ignoring Stella's question.

"Tell us what your company can offer a small business like ours," Jake responded.

Jake and Stella looked at each other, affirming nonverbally that concern for Jade Johnson was off topic for the gentleman. They let it rest and listened to the CEO's presentation of what HR Wellington could offer Legal Grounds, their own small business.

Later that very evening, long after Jake and Stella had completed their business day of legal affairs back at their offices in the coffee shop, and were home, had fed the children, and were readied for bed, Stella received a surprising text message on her phone, from Mrs. Wellington, Daisy Layne.

"Can we meet tomorrow, Wednesday afternoon, for a late lunch?" Daisy texted.

"I'd very much like to do so," Stella jumped at the chance, with a return text, and then added, "What time and where?"

"I'll text you in the morning, with specifics, if that's O.K.," Daisy texted right back.

"Deal. See you tomorrow for late lunch, TBD exact time and place," Stella answered with another text.

"Perfect," Daisy texted.

Stella then turned to Jake, beside her in bed, who was also propped up with pillows, but reading a legal thriller. "You'll never guess who just sent me a text!" she announced with calm anticipation.

Chapter Twenty-Four
Hideaway Haven

Wednesday, October 24th, 8:30 a.m., Daisy texted Stella: Hideaway Haven, 1 p.m., back booth.

Stella was just arriving at her office at Legal Grounds on Wednesday morning, when she noticed her "when-and-where" text from Daisy. The attorney had been checking her phone and expecting all morning this very text, even as she readied her children for school, brought them there, and then continued to her office. It was perfect timing, really, because after she had unlocked her office door and put away her coat, then placed her computer on her desk, she saw a text message was waiting.

Stella had never heard of the Hideaway Haven, which she assumed was a restaurant, and she had no idea of its location. She quickly looked it up on the internet and mapped out directions and drive time. She'd allow for an hour of travel time each way. This place was definitely off the beaten path and not a part of the Sunnyside community. At all.

Stella would also have to inform Jake that he needed to pick up the children from school. If he had meetings, then her mother, Sara, would take them into her home for a visit with Grandma. Stella would contact both her husband and her mom, and the children's school with the notice that she would be unavailable that afternoon. Fortunately, she had a lot of back-up available with her husband and her mom.

"Blessed Lord," Stella whispered a prayer. "Thank you for this wonderful supportive family that we have. We're in this together. We help each other."

At a few minutes before 1 p.m., that very Wednesday afternoon, Stella pulled into the gravel parking lot of the Hideaway Haven Café. Though simple and undecorated, it looked plenty busy, basic, and clean. As she entered, she saw Daisy at a back booth, just as she had indicated in her text.

"I call this my hideaway café, Stella. It's where I come when I just can't take it anymore. Sort of off the grid for me. HR doesn't know about this place. Not good enough for him anyway. Truck stop. That's all it is," Daisy sighed and looked down into her cup of coffee.

"I'm glad you have it figured out," Stella commented quietly. She really just wanted Daisy to talk. Daisy had called her out into the wilderness land of nowhere for this meeting. She had summoned her to a town one block long with a bar and a café and a single gas station with a convenience store. Not even a church here, which was unusual for small-town Iowa. Hideaway Haven was the crossroads of two highways, surrounded by corn and soybean fields, now harvested and dormant. Stella wasn't aware of the reason for the meeting. So, she listened.

There was a pause. The server brought a second cup of coffee, for Stella, and added a whole pot of coffee to the table. As Daisy paused, Stella looked to the front of the café, out the windows at the afternoon sun gleaming off the cars and trucks in the parking lot. She waited.

"They're coming for us, Stella, from Chicago, and I, for one, am going to go clean on this. It's not that I'm innocent. I'm not. However, they will interview me, and I will tell them, everything. It's not a pretty picture. However, since I'll be a witness, I just want to meet with you first, Stella. If anything happens to me, here it is, and here is where they can look. Mind you, I don't need representation. Yet. I'll plead guilty while telling them everything I know. It's that simple. Time to get things right with God and with my conscience, then go to jail," Daisy stopped to catch her breath.

"I'm not sure I know where you're coming from, Daisy," Stella spoke with confusion. "However, I'm willing to sit here and listen."

"That's all that's needed, Stella. Just listen," Daisy said. She again paused and looked down, then looked up right into the eyes of the lawyer, trembling yet somehow relieved.

"Harv and I married later in life, Stella, that's where it all begins for me. He had been married before, twice. It's not difficult for him to land a date, and eventually tie the knot with a wife. He once told me that church women are easy. They all want to get married. However, Harv can be a difficult person to live with behind the scenes. He's busy with his business and gone a great deal. Because of the internet now, we have contracts for doing human resources accounting, benefits, records, etc., all over the Midwest. Harv likes a face-to-face now and then, though. Sometimes more now, than then, if you know what I mean. He travels often. And, seasonally, he golfs with his clients. But really, most of our business can be handled remotely. That is why we were able to move here to Sunnyside and set up shop relatively quickly," Daisy shared.

"That's impressive," Stella noted with admiration.

"To a point," Daisy cautioned. "The reason the first two wives divorced Harvard is that he was cheating on them. All over the countryside, on those trips of his. He had a mistress in every town where he was doing business, it seems. He talks religion and contributes a great deal of money to the church. Frequently, he is on the church board – even as chair. However, how he practices his beliefs is completely another story. He has an eye for younger women and with the amount he contributes to his local church, and the fact that his affairs are out of town, well, he gets away with it."

"That's not right," Stella commented.

"It's evil," Daisy admitted. "Nevertheless, the way things are set up for him in his world, Harvard carries on, and the preacher – with all of the money he pulls in from Harvard – totally looks the other way."

"Why did you marry him?" Stella asked.

"I didn't know about the extra-curricular activities, at first. He said his first and second wives were just difficult people. Harvard swept me off my feet, and I fell for it. Naively and with my own illusion that I was so lucky to marry this guy," Daisy confessed. "But HR knew what he was doing. He knew once I found out, I wouldn't leave, and I wouldn't talk. I'd be a trooper. A go-along-girl. He was right. I went along, didn't leave, and I didn't talk. Until now."

"You put up with a cheating husband?" Stella asked.

"Well, I thought that's what a faithful Christian wife does. Stand by her man and suffer in silence," Daisy acknowledged.

"After all, it's legal and consensual. When it comes to the out-of-town ladies, he has no trouble finding the one-night stands."

"Not Christian, not healthy, not good," Stella observed.

"And that's not where it ends," Daisy explained further. "As Harvard grew older, he still wanted the young ones, but they weren't so keen on him. So, he started this internship initiative in our business. He hired the pretty high school girls…"

"Daisy, now that would be statutory rape, if Harvard has been involved with underage girls," Stella interrupted.

"Well, that's the thing. Some men are not so foolish to become involved with the underage girls, but they can use them as interns, and then groom them for their affairs, later, as soon as they come of age. As soon as they become of legal age, they are still young, innocent, and attractive – and terribly unwise," Daisy explained.

"Now that is sick," Stella shook her head in disgust, with a frown piercing her forehead.

"Oh, these men know what they are doing," Daisy explained.

"What do you mean by 'these men'? I thought we were talking about HR. He is the only man I saw at your corporate headquarters. Who are 'these men'?" Stella inquired.

"HR Wellington's clients. You see, when HR sent Jade Johnson off to Chicago and set her up in a first-rate apartment while she attended the University, he moved her into the position of a full account manager. What Jade didn't know, was that HR promises his accounts in the larger cities that if they sign business contracts with HR Wellington for human resources services – they will receive special benefits. Sign a human resources contract and spend the night with a lovely young college student in her plush apartment. Contracts with benefits," Daisy disclosed.

"Wait, wait. Hold on there," Stella interrupted. "Those are not Jade's values. She would NEVER agree to this! No matter how much money you offered her."

"You are absolutely right, Stella. As a matter of fact, none of the college girls that HR has working as account managers agree to provide the 'bed benefits' for a signed human resources contract. That's where this becomes even more sinister. The customer brings along date rape drugs, and drugs the young woman in her fancy apartment when he serves her wine during their sign-the-contract meeting. Then the customer has his way with the young woman, and leaves. The next day, she really can't figure it all out. If she causes trouble, well, we've moved around a bit. Among the moves, Harvard and his business buddies have been perfecting their strategies of having their way with young beautiful women and keeping their cover. The serial assailant has one big rule to protect himself. He doesn't change his bad behavior, he disguises it. Blend in is his way of life," Daisy spoke in a whisper, face dark with shame.

"This is a jail sentence, Daisy, I hope you realize this," Stella declared. "But Jade's case goes far beyond date rape. It's homicide. She ended up dead in Lake Michigan! Murder!"

"Jade was high class, not easily fooled, and strong in her values," Daisy proclaimed. "Not only was she not fooled into going along with the benefits, she did not respond well to our client the night that she died. The police have done their investigation and I haven't seen their work. But knowing Jade, she refused the wine when the client came to her apartment to sign a contract. There probably was a struggle, and then somehow when he tried to subdue her to receive his benefits, he accidently killed her. That night we received a phone call from the client. He was in big trouble. HR directed him to use the Wellington boat docked in the marina on Lake Michigan. He told this guy to get out some distance on the lake and dispose of her body. Eventually, her body in Lake Michigan surfaced and floated to shore. A passerby found her folded up in a wheeled suitcase. I've been monitoring HR's communications with the client and all of us have been watching the news. That is as much as I know. In any case, this is the end of HR Wellington, both human resources and Harvard Ross. And, the end for me, too, is my guess. I'll be sentenced for my complicity with the business."

"That's dreadful, Daisy – the death of this incredible young woman at the hands of these evil men, and in conjunction with your business, and really, with your knowledge of the assaults on young women over the years," Stella was almost breathless, almost not able to say a word.

"There's a complete video record of what happened in the apartment. That's how they found the client," Daisy continued. "Jade Johnson not only stood up for her values, she had cameras running that night, hidden behind plants in the company apartment. She was one smart young woman, trying to make her way in this world, without support from her family and her church. There was, as they say, a remnant of people that stood with her, mostly the Cheer Squad and their parents.

Having worked with her at our headquarters in Sunnyside, I know what kind of a young woman she was. She did not deserve this. However, through her efforts to protect herself, she has finally brought a stop to HR Wellington, and ended this travesty of a company that was destroying the lives of young women, wherever we did business."

Stella stared in silence.

"One more thing, Stella," Daisy stated with conviction. "I'll say it before you do. I am not even half the woman that Jade Johnson was. I could have stopped this. It got out of hand, yes, but it never should have started in the first place. None of this evil should have happened – the assaults on young women. HR Wellington as a man and HR Wellington as a corporation should never have been predatory over young women who just wanted to enter the business world and be successful. I am the Vice President, and I am a woman, supposedly a Christian woman. I've never cheated on my husband and I don't have affairs. However, this murder and the loss of an innocent, godly and beautiful woman is on me, too. I should have gone to the police long ago about what the older men were doing. You see, I had access to the company apartments which were provided for the young women account managers. I could have planted cameras there, myself, and then gone to the police. In doing so, I could have even sought protection for myself. What was I thinking? I totally failed on this. I, too, am a murderer. I never stepped in to stop this even though I was on the inside track. God have mercy, I am the one who deserves to die. Not Jade. Now that I am willing to work with law enforcement with what I know, it's too late. Jade is gone, because I stood by and did nothing."

* * *

Chapter Twenty-Five
Bonfire and *Out from the Jaws of the Dragon 10: Patty*

(Bonfire opened the final *Out from the Jaws of the Dragon* Friday discourse with reflections about young people who are not appreciated at home.)

With a thrust of two skinny arms, Patty unloaded a pile of books into her locker, Plop! Her shiny blond head disappeared into a tunnel of paper and confusion, hands digging here and there, notebooks flying, coming up for air with a selection of folders and fat textbooks. Then in a sudden burst of gleeful laughter, her eyes sizzled with delight, "Hey Sophia, I'll treat you to a soda at The Grill?"

She paused, coat and homework in tow.

"Nah, not tonight, Patty, I want to get home with my report card."

"Report card? Who gives a care about report cards? My dad is going to lock me up when he sees mine!" and with one kick of a nimble leg, Crash! metal connected with metal, the locker slammed shut. She spun the dial.

Patty and Sophia headed down the hall, with Patty's voice sputtering obscenities, "How can he say anything about my grades? The old man' s a walking drunk tank."

Inside Sophia kicked herself for bringing up the subject of grades. Patty wasn't doing too well in the program - the Fine Arts Magnet within Summer Meadows Junior High. She would barely make it through the year. With her dad's drinking and yelling, she had already decided to give up. Nothing made sense to her, especially not school.

Tiny, bony, fiendish, Patty talked to Sophia, yelled about this 'n that, laughed at her clothes, then patted her on the back, "It don't matter, girl." In class, they were alike, social outsiders ignored by the chatty groups. Out of class, they tagged along with each other in the hallways and occasionally for a few minutes after school. Company. Sophia didn't have to be anything for her. Patty never asked about her family nor did Sophia inquire about hers. Sophia felt that's what held the two together - they both respected the off-limits subjects, which made their exchanges brief.

Unlike Patty, however, Sophia enjoyed their special school program of select students. The two friends were among creative students from the entire county. They were a geeky, high-performing yet rowdy bunch at times - everybody high-energy types, and some very different ones. A girl who thought she was a cat. Eyes gleaming from their sockets like little light bulbs and poising her hands with long white talons ready to pounce, she would sneak up on other students in the library, hissing. Others who just couldn't do enough expression taking it out on the desks, whiteboards, window blinds, marking their imprints on the classrooms. Sophia liked it. School wasn't boring any more. No more playing games with teachers who hated questions. In this group clothes and cliques were not as important as exploration and creativity. Sophia knew Patty and she wouldn't be together long, though. Patty would be out of the program, but Sophia had to work hard, to do the one thing that turned out right at school.

At the door, Sophia's comrade bellowed one last lament, "Prison! Here I go from prison to prison!" and off she went to her tiny stucco house on a busy boulevard.

"See, you," Sophia waved. Somewhere deep down in a hitherto untouched place, Sophia knew how Patty felt but she couldn't say the words. It wasn't Christian to talk like Patty, it wasn't like the Lewis family, it wasn't like their church. The nastiness of Patty's parents and alcohol paralleled the problem of the Lewis family and religion, but it was an unsaid similarity.

Across an open field Sophia met an orange autumn sun, her feet stirring up dust, blazing a trail into the horizon. When Sophia spotted Amy and Kim from her neighborhood sauntering ahead of her, Sophia quickened pace and caught up with them.

"We thought you weren't coming, Sophia, so we started out," Amy began.

"Gosh, what a stack of books you have, and on the night of the dance . . .," Kim observed.

"Oh, I'm not going, I mean, I'll be busy at home tonight, other things to do," Sophia's words floated away as Kim and Amy continued to discuss their plans for the evening.

Rounding the corner at the end of the block, the girls crunched leaves like cornflakes, three abreast on the sidewalk. As they kicked up the leaves, Kim zeroed in on Sophia's shoes, "Good grief, Sophia, what happened to your shoes?"

Reluctantly Sophia glanced down at the broken leather or vinyl or whatever, strapped brown shoes that were now red, sort of. Red in the split corners anyway. Bought used, the shoes were now cracked from wear. After an endeavor to disguise them with shoe polish - the only polish Sophia could find in the house, a reddish-brown paste that didn't cover up anything, the shoes were now two-toned. Luckily, Sophia thought, the hole in the sole of the bottom, patched with cardboard, was not visible. With the right shoe patched, and the left re-colored, the pair did not match.

"Well, I wanted them this way, you know, psychedelic shoes," Sophia returned.

Satisfied, Kim turned away and stayed on the topic of fashion, "Amy, I like your boots "

"These are my sister' s boots from last year, but almost new."

"Gosh, I would not be caught dead in my older sister's old boots, but then she would probably destroy them before passing them on. My mom is taking me out one of these days to get mine. "

Kim stopped talking. No one talked until the threesome reached her house.

"See you guys tonight; oh yeah, Sophia, you're got to work on school stuff. Too bad. That's what you get for being such a freak. Too bad you weren't blessed with being like us normal folks."

Amy and Sophia waved her off and waited for a green light. The conversation hesitated while the two crossed traffic, then Amy began to explain Kim.

"You have to understand her, Sophia. She's the middle one with an older sister who does everything right, a younger sister who doesn't have to do anything to be right, and then there's Kim. You just have to take her for who she is."

"Yeah, I know. Parents these days are something else," Sophia replied with courtesy, but the conversation didn't make sense to her. Bewildered, Sophia couldn't feel the family stuff, unable to even figure out what was going on at her own house with her family.

When the girls discussed boys, clothes, make-up, and piercings, Sophia was unable to grasp what the fuss was all about. It was not easy to be interested in the things that Mr. Lewis hated, and Mrs. Lewis mocked. The girls acted like Sophia was out of touch, but Sophia didn't have enough energy to pursue these interests and to contest home on them. Sophia had life to think about - the problem of what to do about living.

"By the way, how did you do on your report card?" Amy interrupted Sophia's thoughts.

"A's."

"A's, all A's? They put you in those special classes and you still get all A's?"

"It doesn't' t matter," Sophia said, "grades don't mean nothing anyway. By the way, did you get your new ice skates yet?

Won't be long and it'll be cold enough to skate." Sophia had lied and changed the subject. Grades did matter. She felt they were all she had.

After Amy and Sophia parted, Sophia felt the wind chill the back of her neck. The sun was still beaming golden rays, but they were not keeping the wind away. Senses dulled to the weather, Sophia reached inside her pocket and fingered her report card envelope. This had been an exceptionally good fall quarter despite the shoes, second-hand clothes, and lack of friends. The grades were amazing more to her than anyone. Maybe she could be someone, she wondered. It had been worth it, all the embarrassment and ridicule. On paper at least, she felt she was legitimate.

Sophia wondered if she would be able to make it as a person in the world. Would she ever fit in, be warm, be fed, be close without invasion, be loved? If she could study and be a good student, maybe someday her parents would respect and take care of her, too, Sophia reasoned. The report cards were her tickets to the train out of rejection. Sophia clutched them - official, valid, approving - and trusted them to transcend to her home life and make her a worthy person, someone who could be loved. With excited hope, Sophia walked home.

After dinner Sophia flew to her room, then bounced back into the kitchen to catch her mom, Mrs. Lewis, alone.

"Mom, you'll never guess what I have to share with you. The surprise of your life!" and Sophia carefully set the report card packet on the counter next to her mother. Her thoughts intensified watching her mother open the white folder with official school lettering.

Mrs. Lewis slowly looked at each subject with curiosity and no other outward response. Placing the cards back into the envelope, Mrs. Lewis paused, took a breath, looked her daughter directly in the eye, and carefully chose her words. "Sophia," she said quietly.

"Yes," Sophia answered with anticipation.

"You are to never again bring home your report cards," Mrs. Lewis said.

Stunned, Sophia steadied herself.

Mrs. Lewis continued, "Do you think Mark and Molly earn grades like these? And they work very hard at school. They try. Do you want the twins to stop trying? It will be your fault if they do not do well in school. Why of all the nerve!" Firmness was transformed to rage radiating from Mrs. Lewis' face.

Blood was gushing into Sophia's head ready to burst, abhorring her wickedness, the evil life that couldn't do right by living but couldn't die. Again, Sophia was destroying the family, again Sophia was ruining her mom's life. Not only would the report cards have to be burned, the evil mind and body also.

Desperate to please her mom, ardent to redeem itself, Sophia's confused mind raced. If only the grades would not hurt her family and in the end be worth something, maybe then her mom would love her, too. Education, a profession, and a job, Sophia decided, but she would have to keep the grades to herself, and her future plans a secret. Each good grade would be a ticket to somewhere in the future. Sophia would have to learn how to get a respectable job and take care of herself, she decided. Maybe then, she would finally deserve love from her family.

The problem, Sophia deduced, was that her mom had to take care of her. Sophia had been forced upon her by the fluke of her unwanted birth. But if Sophia could be self-supporting, then maybe her mom would receive her daughter with a mother' s open arms of love and respect. As Mrs. Lewis turned and left the kitchen, Sophia held onto her report cards and her hope for a chance, the chance to live and be loved.

Chapter Twenty-Six
Bonfire and *Out from the Jaws of the Dragon 11: Mistrust*

(Bonfire Books continued, discussing what is unseen in a community and what is actually acknowledged.)

Footsteps rumbled at the back door, stomping out snow on the rug in the back hallway. From the family room, Sophia clicked off the television with the remote, got up from the couch, and met her Aunt Carrie and Uncle Neil as they came out of the kitchen into the dining room of their plush and modern new home. Auntie slipped off her fur coat and draped it over the tall back of a dining room chair.

"How did things go, Sophia?" Carrie asked as she propped open her purse on the table.

"Fine, we played until Brittany and Ethan went to bed at eight. They went right to sleep. Did you and Uncle Neil have a good time?"

Aunt Carrie addressed her husband, "Neil, you sure did. Would you hand me your wallet, Dear?"

Neil mumbled and reached into his back pocket as he set his coat over the edge of the table.

"Fortunately, I did the driving home tonight," Aunt Carrie chuckled. "Boys will be boys, especially at the country club party."

Sophia didn't know Neil and Carrie and their little family well. They had recently moved into the area, but she knew that in the extended family, Neil (an outsider who married in) was considered a winner. Professional, young, and charming, he was hailed as a worthy catch for Mrs. Lewis' sister. Aunt Carrie and Uncle Neil had started their family and were settling into a solid middle-class neighborhood. They had sharp tastes and high ambitions for the good life: money, family, society.

After Aunt Carrie paid Sophia for the night of babysitting, she motioned to Sophia's backpack which was still sitting in the far corner of the family room. "Neil, would you show Sophia her room upstairs? I'm going to pop in and check on the children."

Aunt Carrie left for the nursery, next to the master bedroom on the main floor. Uncle Neil picked up the backpack from the corner.

As Neil passed Sophia, heading for the upstairs, she could smell the effects of his partying. She followed her uncle up a tall open staircase, passed a chandelier, and down a long hallway to the last upstairs bedroom. Her uncle set the teen's backpack on the floor and planted himself on the bed, facing Sophia and a ray of light beaming in from the hallway. Sophia halted in the doorway, not entering the room, staring, waiting for her uncle's departure. When she didn't move, Neil extended his arms, "Come sit on my lap, Sophia."

Without responding, Sophia still waited for him to leave, and searched for a point of reference. What could he want? Why didn't he leave?

"I'm going to wish you good night," Neil stated.

Confused, fearful, passive, Sophia still waited, standing motionless while trying to figure out what to do. She didn't have to ponder long.

Uncle Neil leaned forward, outstretched his long arms, and grabbed Sophia into his lap, kissing her mouth with his lips and plunging into her mouth his tongue. The man's breath was heavy with alcohol, and his teeth were shaking.

Sophia numbed, floppy like a ragdoll, and Neil continued and quickened his pace. Lifting the teen off his lap, he placed her flat on her back on the bed. Bending over, Neil unfastened the teen's clothes in front, then reached around and unfastened her undergarment in the back, exposing her upper torso to his face and lips. He put his head to the teen's exposed body, sucking like a predator, breathing heavily, licking, mouthing, pawing, pulling, and inhaling the teen inside of him. She was horrified.

Then the man's face moved downward and as he did so, he unzipped the teen's jeans in front, with shaking but firmly-directed movements. Pulling her jeans down, the man bared just enough to massage between the teen's legs with the same shaking but steady and strong, compulsive and forceful fingers. He penetrated the teen with his large fingers.

The man massaged deeply, plundering, reaching down inside, splitting open Sophia's insides.

"Help me, God," her brain cried out, but as with Mr. Lewis all those years, Sophia was deadly silent and terrified as a fearful non-participant.

The man was cutting and shredding her, opening the path for his final full body plunge. Neil held onto Sophia with one hand, while he pulled something out of his pants with his other hand. He moved one of his large hands to ready himself, steadying his extended organ, upright and prepared, and aiming for the path to the teen, his final goal. The man was on the verge of the summit of his attack.

Suddenly Neil backed away, adjusted his pants, turned around, and bolted out of the room.

At that point, Sophia felt she was not in the bed, but had been watching what was happening in helpless terror from overhead. She dared not be present in her body which lay disconnected, dead to her, on the bed. She dared not enter the refuse destroyed by a violent terrorist assault.

The teen's eyes were wide open, staring at the doorway, a beam of light yet coming in from the hall, afraid that if there were any movement, the predatory man would return. She was fearful that any activity would be a catalyst for further hostility, just like with her dad at home. Finally, after several hours, Sophia felt that she could enter only the hands of the body by reaching out her hand to the sheets and blanket to pull them over, without feeling, without making direct contact with the body, without her touching her, not dressing, not undressing. She found the body quivering, vacillating between numbness and a deluge of feelings of grotesqueness. Her eyes never shut but remained wide open as she lay paralyzed staring at the ceiling, then the door, trying to forget, in dread of the possibility of the assailant's return.

In the early hours of a dark winter morning, Sophia arose alone, put her things together, dressed without acknowledging the body was hers, and slipped out of the house unnoticed. As she brushed by coats yet strewn on chairs in the dining room, the odor of liquor still lingered overhead. She could smell the uncle's breath, feel his smelly shaking teeth, the command of his forceful and direct long fingers, his invading body like an atomic bomb attacking an unsuspecting peaceful place.

Sophia's insides resisted feeling. She didn't know what he had been doing. He knew she didn't know, he knew she wasn't watching, he knew she wasn't prepared, he knew she did not know what to do. It had been an ambush of guerrilla warfare. Now there were scars, bombs planted in the body, the body a minefield. Each time the body was acknowledged, was touched, an explosion went off. She was terrified.

Since it was Sunday morning and Sophia knew her way around the city, she caught a bus to go to church. She made footprints in fresh-fallen snow all the way to a bus stop, her backpack strapped over her shoulder. In a misty fog, crystalized trees contrasted black bark and white snow, but inside the teen black and white were meshed to gnarly grey. Slowly Sophia walked and found her way, killing time, conscious of anyone looking at her, wondering if they knew.

At church Sophia donned her mask of steel determination, long perfected after her father's advances. Yet she was mentally mortified and petrified, sitting in the back pew alone. Choir ladies of sleepy powdered faces (lit up with make-up), marched by, eyes rolling from mounted hymnal to the right, back to the hymnal, then to the left, glancing, taking attendance of the crowd; an eye targeted Sophia. She wondered what the woman saw. Did she know what had happened? Could she tell?

At the back of the church, Sophia slipped out and went to the restroom to stare long and hard into the mirror, detached from body, rejecting feeling, trying to rid the body of what had happened. It would not go away. In the mirror, her eyes were hollow to look at, yet they penetrated the rubble, the bombed-out refuse of a savage attack. Confusing questions worked over her mind: Why had this uncle picked her out? What was written on her face: rubbish, ready to trash? How did this uncle know it was O.K. to do this? He was not a blood relative in either Doug's or Bethany's extended family. He was not born into either of the two networks of evil that she knew too well, the networks full of men that preyed on underage girls and women that looked the other way. This man had married into the family from the outside. Did this mean that any man from anywhere could do as he wished with her? Not just the blood-relative men at home but any man in the world, anyone who should perchance cross her path? Sophia's body belonged to them, too? Men owned girls, and their women sadistically accused the child? They could just have their way, whenever, wherever, with whomever? They all had power?

Returning in time for the sermon, Sophia could hear from a distance the preacher. "Give your life to Christ, let him be the Lord of your life. He will save you, he will rule you."

Lord of a person's life, give oneself over. There wasn't much left to give. But giving herself over Sophia understood well. If the pastor would have said, "Be yourself," she never would have known what he meant because she could no longer feel herself. There was no self that was left to be; self was wrapped up in her dad, in her uncles, in the needs of her mom. "Deny yourself," was the mandate from God.

Yes, Sophia knew how to deny herself, submit, yield, give up, commit herself - it was Christian to be without self, to have no will. To will was to sin, so her will was submitted and denied as she abdicated to godly parents, to godly relatives, to the pastor who wanted her to keep silent, to the church that also seemed to say, "Do not tell or you are evil, with a lying and perverse tongue. Christians do not say those things, especially about their parents, their own family."

The pastor continued, "Commit your day to God, always beginning with prayer and by reading your Bible, first thing in the morning, even if it is just one verse. Begin with God, give him priority."

Sophia was coming near to having read the entire Bible, along with fasting and praying on behalf of her family as Nehemiah had in the Old Testament for his countrymen.

The pastor concluded with, "Release yourself to God. He wants your life, he wants you."

Later, at Sunday School, Sophia's church friend Ruthie commented while pointing a long and polished fingernail to the back of Sophia's leg, "There's a tear in your leggings, Sophia."

"Yes, maybe it happened on the way here," Sophia surmised while she cowered and shuffled her legs, hiding her strategy of wearing everything worn and as long as possible, while stretching babysitting money.

"Oh, I just thought you'd want to know," Ruthie added.

"Thanks, Ruthie," Sophia answered.

The Lewis family came later and sat together at a subsequent church service, all lined up across a pew. From the corner of Sophia's eye, she peered at her mother, searching her aspect for clues as to how and what to tell her about the previous night. Sitting facing the pastor who just last summer had made it clear not to tell her mother about her father, Sophia concluded that surely, she could tell her mother about this uncle – the brother-in-law who was not blood-related family. Surely this would not break up her parents' marriage. Auntie Carrie was her mother's sister, but Uncle Neil did not have blood ties, Sophia reasoned. Looking again at her mother, Sophia could feel her mother's presence. Her mother would know how to handle her sister and her sister's husband, the girl hoped.

Sunday evening at home, doing homework, Sophia wrestled with the words it would take to talk with her mother. She knew that if she didn't gather the courage to take care of this tonight, she would never find the resolve to make it happen in the future. After less than twenty-four hours, the assault already seemed like a nightmare, a shadow. It refused to come into the light, but it remained a shadow that that would cling to Sophia and would blacken her being forever.

On a piece of lined notebook paper Sophia wrote a note telling her mom that "Uncle Neil took my clothes off last night and did things."

After scrawling her name at the bottom, Sophia folded the note several times, dashed to the living room, flung it over the newspaper her mother was reading to land it in her lap, and escaped back upstairs to her bedroom.

A few minutes later, that seemed like a day later, Sophia saw her mother standing at her bedroom doorway with a stern look on her face.

Slowly Sophia turned to face her mom, as Mrs. Lewis sat down on her bed. The two were alone and silence hovered a while before anything was said. The mother stared at her daughter, long and hard.

"Did he take his clothes off also?" Mrs. Lewis asked.

"He started to, then he pulled them up and ran out of the room," Sophia answered.

"Where was Aunt Carrie when this was going on?" Mrs. Lewis asked.

"Checking on Ethan and Brittany," Sophia answered.

"Does she know?" Mrs. Lewis continued with clarifying questions.

"No, I don't think so," Sophia replied.

"Have you shared this with anyone else?" Mrs. Lewis asked.

"No, I thought I'd better talk with you," Sophia admitted, and then glanced away, shuddering at the thought of talking with anyone else about what had happened.

Silence again. Then Mrs. Lewis' brow sharpened to a rigid frown. "Well, Sophia, it's lucky you only told me about this, because you are lying, and I would have to punish you for even more lying and ruining an upright and good man who married into our family."

Sophia didn't look up.

"You, Sophia, are a liar, a wicked liar." Mrs. Lewis emphasized. "I do not believe you, but you do not have to go over to their house again. And, you are to never tell anyone about this – spreading your lies. Do you understand that, young lady?"

Sophia finally looked at her mom and responded with a quiet, "Yes." Her eyes were burning with tears. Why had she once again displeased her mom? Her heart sank. She accused herself and was determined to cut out the pain on her insides. The pain from this uncle, the pain from displeasing her mom, the tormented body wanting to extinguish itself.

Nothing happened, Sophia told herself, and she disconnected herself from the grotesque feelings inside, and called them the liars. She vowed to do the best she could and when she did, she decided, someday maybe her mom would love her and call Sophia her own.

Chapter Twenty-Seven
Bonfire and *Out from the Jaws of the Dragon 12: New Creation*

(Bonfire Books concluded their final exchange about the novella with ideas about how they could support and encourage the young people in their community.)

At a Christian retreat center, light rippled through a rectangular next-to-ceiling window, into a darkened bunk room. Vaguely Sophia could see the form of bunkbeds around her on three sides, including her own bunk, three sets in all, six girls to their room. Everyone was in for the night.

The snores and sighs of Sophia's five camp companions patterned harmoniously into a quiet buzz. Breathing - weaving. Soon Sophia would no longer interrupt the weave or break the harmony, the pattern. Soon she would be different no more. Soon Sophia would no longer be.

The church girls were away on retreat for the weekend at a camp not far from civilization, about a two-hour bus ride into the mountains. After school in the afternoon, they had gathered at church, then rode into seclusion in time for pizza and an evening of games, laughter, and middle school verbalisms and antics. Sophia had hung around the girls she knew well, not knowing what to say (as usual), but smiling politely to be friendly, to be accepted, to belong, to blend in. In return, the other girls laughed. They knew Sophia didn't know how to interact. Sophia knew they knew, and once in a while, they let her know.

"Don't be so sensitive, we're only kidding," the girls would giggle.

Kidding, Sophia thought. Right. Then she would laugh, too. Inside, it did not feel funny.

The planned activities ended with hot chocolate and brownies around a fire in the fireplace of the great hall of the retreat center. Sophia knew better than to eat milk and chocolate, but she did anyway, and a stomachache followed. Quietly, she had put on her winter jacket for a short walk in the subzero night air. The winterized camp was basically one building perched on a jagged cliff high above a lake. Tomorrow, intermingled with Bible study, the students would have ample opportunity for sledding, skating, and skiing.

The walk was short, there wasn't much to see, and the cold quickly penetrated her outdoor clothes. Inside, she headed for her room in the girls' section, running into their youth pastor, Chuck, as she crossed the great hall. Sophia had not frequently interacted with Chuck one-to-one, but she knew from a particular conversation that he was pretty laid back. Once she had called him and asked what she could do to stop banging her head against cement. It hurt afterwards, headaches and such, but Sophia couldn't seem to stop. At the moment, the cement seemed to relieve pain, but later her head would throb.

Chuck advised Sophia not to worry about it. "When I get angry or frustrated," he confessed, "I break pencils. I try not to let it bother me. When you are not hurting anyone, why feel guilty?" Chuck had said.

This night Chuck smiled easily, "Leaving us so soon? The fun is just starting; besides, you don't want brownies for breakfast, Sophia."

Returning the smile, she tried to think of what to say, "Well, not really."

They both kept walking, opposite directions.

Sitting on her lower bunk, Sophia removed her shoes and unrolled her sleeping bag, nestling in, fully dressed. Facing the wall, with her eyes sealed, she rehearsed over and over a plan. The others would be in later, there was time to think, and in the night, life loomed before Sophia as a giant. It was the problem of being, that is, tons and tons of existence.

Questions, yes; at home Sophia had searched for answers night after night reading into the dawn, staying awake, guarding the night, seeking an acceptable place for her life. From the Greek classics, then through the Middle Ages, she read history and philosophy, the questions and queries, finally landing smack dab in the middle of modern existentialism. Home. Angst. The question of being, of failure, of a life she found impossible to live. There had been no choice. She was. She did not want to be. This was not a life desired. This was not a life to be lived. It should not have been. The intellectual questions raised by the philosophers did not remain questions in her mind for long. She had to find answers, so she could go on living. The existentialists made her feel right at home and wanted, particularly the ones who said the final road to peace out of the angst was in death. Without fear, death became the ultimate goal if the paths ahead were to be unrelenting torment. The message of anxiety was not new to her, she felt it every day.

There were no answers in life it seemed, save to declare existence non-existent, and this was not always successful. Defeating numbness, feelings pursued and eventually found her, transcending denial. It was then that peace through death recurred in her mind like a pounding heartbeat ever reminding her that if there were no way out in living, death would provide the ultimate escape. It was especially comforting to reflect on the fact that death would be a decision and action, a solution she could carry out herself, on her own, without interference or influence. Like Chuck had said, "Why worry when you are hurting no one." It was the one good and sensible choice she could make. She could solve her problem. She could take responsibility and stop ruining everyone's lives.

Secretly, Sophia would take control of her body, her life, and her final destiny. What lay beyond death was another question she had considered. It seemed death was an open door to peace, to rest, as opposed to the anxiety of being meat in a cage with a wolf or with wolves. The responsibility of guarding this life had been too great for her and she had failed many times over.

This night from a lower bunk in the woodland retreat, she contemplated the end, visualizing the path to peace, the steep icy cliff dropping from outside the back door of the center. The drop-off would provide the leap to safety. A walk in the night, an accidental slip, a fall to the ice below, then unconsciousness until exposure to the elements finished the job. Simple, clean, no note, no blame, just quietly step away from failure.

Her mother hating accomplishment, her father hating autonomy - they would not have to hate any longer. The one social outlet her father allowed, the church youth group, would no longer be disconcerted. At summer camp, though Sophia was an avid swimmer, she had had the wrong color bathing suit. Sitting among the girls this very night with her silent smile, she couldn't think of what to say. Her attendance seemed to interfere with the process of everyone else growing up. She got in the way, and she couldn't figure out how to change. What was she supposed to be? What was wrong with this person? How could she learn so much at school and not square with being, with her very existence?

Sophia's friends came in late, around midnight, giggling their way to bed, joking about the boys of their church group. They quickly went to sleep after talking had ceased. Sophia nulled her presence so as not to draw attention, so as not to bother anyone. In resolute silence she waited for the night to pass, for her opportunity.

At two a.m., the night felt deep, intense, and seemed to welcome her plan. Strategy was interrupted, however, by an inaudible voice, imprinting a message inside of her.

"Sophia, I want you, I want your life, the life you are ready to end. I promise to take the life and transform it for you, to transform you."

The voice Sophia recognized from reading through the Bible recently. He was the someone who had created man and woman, then taken Israel as his own, providing a Savior for all of humanity, and establishing a plan for eternity. What had most caught her attention in reading the Bible was what she couldn't shake off now. He loved Israel, he loved his creation, he loved the very ones who had rejected his own son, Jesus.

"I love you, Sophia, I want you to be my child."

Trembling, Sophia buried into her pillow her once resolute head, now slowly oozing fat tears out of pain and sorrow-soaked eyes. Her insides were captivated and embraced by the historical love relationship of God and Israel. The Old Testament flashed before her as a film, and she recalled how God had not given up on the ones who had repeatedly wandered away from and even openly rejected him. From Genesis to Revelation, the Bible was a Love Promise between God and those who received him.

Did she know this God of love? She'd have to find him, to let him know her. He said he loved her; she had to find out if the words in the Bible were meant for her, also. Surely the Israelites had tremendous family problems and God accepted them. They were no more a fragment of humanity than Sophia, herself. Through Ezekiel, God had spoken an allegory of how he picked up an unwanted babe from the gutter; then from the discard he created a powerful and beautiful people. Did God really want her life? She had no answer, but based on history, this was plausible. Hungering him, craving the chance for rebirth, Sophia responded and answered the voice she heard calling her.

"O God, I've failed. Do you desire failure? Trash? Can you rescue someone as far gone as this vile flesh? Are you a big enough God?" Again, the stories of the Bible came to Sophia's mind, when God's arm had been strong enough to deliver even the most hopeless.

More tears. "I want to trust you, God. I'm afraid." He wasn't her father, or was he? She thought about the God of the Bible and about her dad, Mr. Lewis. The complete message of the Bible, she sensed, was a world apart from her father's teachings. God never forced His way. He never demanded. He was a provider, not a thief.

God was not now forcing his way into her life. He was asking. He was waiting with gentility and neither pressure nor violation of her will. He would not cross the line of her will and come unwelcomed. God respected boundaries. Separation. He presented an invitation. He was promising to make things right. He was a gentleman.

Sophia knew from reading the Bible that the complete rebirth required complete trust and commitment on her part. She had to decide if she was willing to be vulnerable to the God who was personally, intimately speaking to her. Her being, her inner voice trembled yet answered, "Yes, God."

The girl tumbled into the Father's arms. He was now her Shepherd and together they began a pilgrimage from complicated evil and confusion to freedom and peace. As she embarked on the journey, the girl rested in the Father's promises with, what some would call unrealistic faith and hope. She rested, unaware that the battle for truth and reality was only beginning. The Lord provided green pastures for his lamb, his child, by the waters of rest. At the same time, a tempest brewed about them.

In the end, this is how Sophia knew what love was: Jesus Christ laid down his life for her. God was her one true Father, and his son Jesus was her Messiah, her Savior. Through Jesus, God took responsibility for evil; Sophia no longer needed to be afraid.

Jesus brought Sophia into being, he desired the best for her, he saved her, he brought her into grace. Jesus brought Sophia into light, he was light. Jesus exposed what had happened in darkness and birthed her new life when she accepted his loving, healing touch.

"Therefore, if anyone is in Christ, he is a new creation; old things have passed away; all things have become new," came true for the little girl.

It was Jesus who was with the little girl in her deepest childhood agony, who kept a person alive inside the body of a benumbed girl. It was Jesus who whispered into her heart, "I made you, I want you," when as a faltering young woman, she was ready to pull the plug and halt her life. It was Jesus who restored her and continued healing even when the pit of evil seemed deep and dark beyond the reach of God's loving grasp.

Jesus loved the little girl, his very own creation.

He did not pass by the plundered girl tossed to the side of the road, the unloved girl left to die. Moreover, Jesus did not just bring the child psychology, or theology, or education, or medicine, or government, or laws, or any type of organization, institution, protest, or placard. He did not bring only words or remedies or programs.

Jesus picked up the child and wrapped the child in the Father's love.

Because doctors, psychologists, theologians, lawyers, educators, the government, and organizations, programs, institutions, protests, and placards were not love. Nor could they force a mother, like they could not force the little girl's mom, to love her child. Nor were they able to prevent the little girl's dad from plundering his own, his children. And experts and institutions were unable to repair the damage.

Jesus was the Shepherd who laid down his life for his lamb. The little girl would not want.

* * *

Chapter Twenty-Eight
Jake and Stella: Night Terrace

Friday, October 26th, 9 p.m. Night intern texted Jake & Stella: Officers on the way.

Jake didn't see the text at first, nor did Stella; their phones were buried among their things, some place. And, in any case, they were in their Friday night wonderland already. They had a lot to share, however, first, they just wanted to enjoy each other's company. They were snuggled together on the comfy couch in front of the fireplace in their master bedroom, at home. However, though they opted to spend the night in their own quarters, Grandma Sara and Cowboy Jack had welcomed the grandchildren into their home in the countryside, once again, for a special night with the grandparents at their ranch. In the morning, whenever that would be, Jake was planning to fix breakfast and serve Stella in bed. Saturday morning special. He wanted his wife to know how remarkable she was, how much he loved her.

Earlier in the evening, Bonfire Books had completed reading and discussing, *Out from the Jaws of the Dragon.* They had finished October on the high note of the novella about a plundered child, who, in the end, finds her Savior. The sequel, *Into the Hands of God,* also by Taylor O'Brien, would be considered at some point for another month, but not right away. The club members needed time to contemplate what they had learned from the first book.

For the book club gathering that night, Stella had brought Travis the intern back in, paying him extra cash, as an evening worker for the final Friday in October. He served refreshments to the club members during their closing meeting of the autumn month.

After the club members had all left, Stella instructed Travis to clean up, then set the alarm, lock the doors, and finally, to stop by Cowboy Jack's to drop off the keys. The Wild Mustang Corral had topnotch security, so she was not worried about Travis working alone, then locking up, and bringing the keys across the horseshoe-shaped mall to her father's night manager at Cowboy Jack's. It was dark, yes, but the mall was well-lit and busy, the weather was still nice, and Travis knew what he was doing.

Nevertheless, eventually there was trouble that brewed that night at the Wild Mustang Corral, in full view of Travis, quietly working solo behind-the-scenes at Legal Grounds with the lights turned down low. In the end, he had deposited the trash out the back, turned out the interior lights from the rear hallway, and was coming up front to set the alarm and let himself out the front door, and then lock it.

As Travis walked toward the front, facing the all glass floor-to-ceiling windows, he noticed two characters outside, on the other side of the glass, poised opposite each other in the night on the otherwise empty front terrace. The silhouettes of their figures were black against the flood lights of the Corral. But they weren't silent shapes. The two were screaming and yelling. Violently.

Apparently, the couple hadn't noticed that Travis had been left behind to clean up. Anyway, they were each seated at opposing sides of a table on the deserted night terrace, addressing each other at the top of their lungs. At first, Travis could not understand what they were yelling, for the most part. However, he perceived that on his right was a woman, middle-aged, and on his left was a man, also middle-aged. Their stature and their voices gave away their age and their genders.

Travis paused, then ducked in behind the front counter, peeking his eyes up over this barrier to see and hear what was happening. It appeared that at this age, the couple was old enough to know better. He texted Jake, then Stella, with no response. Again. However, he didn't have to wait long to begin to perceive what was taking place out there on the night terrace, somewhat.

The man yelled, "How dare you go to the police! They are never going to believe you! You traitor, you evil woman! You benefitted more than anyone from Wellington Inc., and now you are going to betray this lucrative company. You are going to drag my name right into the dirt. What happened that night was an accident! No one meant any harm to that girl!"

The woman responded, "You can tell that to the detectives tomorrow! But they have video proof, both from her apartment and from the marina! That was a company boat you had your guy use to dump the body after he killed her. You never even reported her missing. It was a kill and cover up from the get-go. If it weren't for her friends filing the missing person's report, they may not have even been able to identify her naked body. We're all going down this time! At least I can be a witness, but it's too little, too late. I should have stopped it! And saved her life and protected the others! I'm going to be arrested, too, you know. I should have reported you as a predator, ruining innocent young ladies - long before a respectable girl ended up dead! That's where your evil deeds have taken us! Murder! We are murderers now!"

The man shot back, "You want murder? I'll show you murder, woman!"

At the word murder, the large man, enraged, got to his feet, then vaulted up onto the table and stood over the woman. In his blackened silhouette, in the shadows, his right arm was deep in his right pocket, with his hand inside and pointing something through his righthand pocket. He was aiming what seemed to be a pocketed weapon directly at the woman, while cursing her, threatening her, damning her.

The much smaller woman screamed, bolted up also, but cowered under the man, and then reeled back. In an instant, she pulled something shiny out of her righthand pocket, into the open, in plain sight, under the night lights.

The man quickly reacted by pulling his right hand out of his pocket, and then displaying his handgun which reflected metallic light into the night. Would he fire? Would he attack? Would he leap down from the table and smash her body against the floor of the stone terrace?

Just then there was a flash!

The man, indeed, crashed down, his body hitting the edge of the table at an angle, his head going down hard and further to the ground, smashing against the slate terrace floor, barely missing landing on the woman. She, in turn, collapsed on the cold stone surface, like a rag doll, weeping and sobbing.

Travis immediately called for emergency services, "There's been an incident here on the front terrace of Legal Grounds. We need an ambulance," he said, then added, "and police officers. These people are armed and firing their weapons – at each other."

He then tried Stella and Jake again, with no response, again.

Within minutes an ambulance and several patrol cars arrived. Travis unlocked the front door to let a sergeant in. The EMTs were busy with the body of the man, and the weeping woman.

"What's going on here?" he asked. "Where are Jake and Stella, the owners?"

At that moment, Jake and Stella came rushing up from their speedily parked car, in their sweats and slip-on shoes. They had finally seen the texts and immediately left for the coffee shop.

Travis told the story of what he saw, in detail, about the woman and the man arguing on the terrace. The man lunged at the woman pointing what turned out to have been a gun in his right hand, initially stowed away but pointing through his right pocket. The woman freaked out in fear and pulled out her own handgun into the open, under the night lights. There had been a flash from one of the guns, and now the man was dead. The woman was alive but hysterical.

After hearing the intern's story, Jake and Stella looked at each other with serious expressions and discerning eyes. One of them said, "The woman is going to need a good lawyer," and the other nodded, answering, "Yes."

Epilogue

Sunnyside learned a lesson. A predator can hide in plain sight in a noble society. The predator's goal is to camouflage his or her activity while grooming a community to look the other way. This is the predator's modus operandi in order to have access to the most innocent, the most vulnerable.

The Chamber of Commerce continued without the Wellingtons. Ms. Pearson and her Sunnyside Media Team began producing their podcast featuring Sunnyside as a glowing family and business community.

Owen and Willow of O WOW! Travel led their boating party excursion in Europe, exploring the literature of Mary Shelley (*Frankenstein*) and the innovation of Earl Bakken (Medtronic).

Bonfire Books read a book a month with discourse on Friday nights at the Legal Grounds Café. Eventually the book club read the second novella of Taylor O'Brien's series about positive solutions and personal triumph, *Into the Hands of God.*

The O WOW! Travel expedition and the Bonfire readings comprise the next novel in the *Legal Grounds* Series:

Independent Inquiry